DEATH IMPRESSIONS

A NOVEL

J L REHMAN

PARTNERS IN CRIME PUBLISHERS

A Division of Rehman Technology Services, Inc.
34646 Rust Road
Eustis, FL, 32736

COVER DESIGNED BY J L REHMAN

Manufactured in the United States of America

ISBN: 978-1-60771-001-1

www.partnersincrimepublishers.com

For Dr. William Donnelly

CONTENTS

a little misunderstanding................................... 1

dead fish 7

shaving prunes... 9

predisposition 14

malathion cocktail..................................... 19

palm spikes... 30

keep the change.. 39

felons, hamburger and pine sol......................... 46

post traumatic stress.................................. 56

moldy addictions...................................... 65

animal police 72

dreams in the freezer................................. 78

black eyed hurricane................................... 89

what dead guy?.. 96

strike a pose... 100

clothing optional..................................... 109

white trash drama 118

chiggers... 126

happy hour... 133

an elusive reality... 141

sharp tools.. 145

a small slice of... 155

a tight fit... 162

handcuffed frozen chicken.................................. 170

bubble wrapped silence...................................... 178

miami vice... 183

cake mix.. 190

stretched perspective.. 193

and the winner is... 201

you really don't want to know.............................. 203

no coupons.. 212

ladies night 215

a perfect execution... 227

GYOTAKU: Japanese from *gyo* "fish" + *taku* "rubbing" a form of art dating from the 1800's originally used by fishermen to record their catches.

By placing the "subject" on a flat surface and painting one side with *sumi* ink, a piece of rice paper is carefully applied on top of the subject and is pulled off with a mirror image created on the paper.

Joe Salas, whether by accident or inspiration, created *"Death Impressions."*

a little misunderstanding

"SHE STRUNG ME ALONG for over a year," Joe had blurted. "Where's *my* one-man show? Know where? Right in this cruddy bucket of water, that's where!" Lydia didn't know how bad he wanted it. Yes, she did. He'd told her. She didn't care. He wasn't going to let the spinster bitch get away with it.

"This is not," Lydia hissed, "the time or place!" Her elderly Botox-petrified skin stretched into a lopsided sneer as she desperately tried to smile at her art gallery clients already heading for the door.

So, okay, she didn't see the humor in his standing with one hand wrapped around the mop handle and the other in the air like a lost prophet, eyes wide, all teeth. And, okay, he did announced to a room full of clients that featured artist, Furguson Novello, had been arrested for counterfeiting art work. But then Joe had said he gotten off. But couldn't resist adding, "On a *technicality*." Sure, it was all a lie, but the best he could come up with on such short notice.

Not the time or place? "Just as good a time as any!" Joe had gripped the mop with both hands and announced, "What do you say folks? Don't leave—we're just getting started." He'd flailed the mop across the hardwood floor as if to cut them off at the ankles.

Their reactions, mouths open in shock, too frightened to know what to do next. Screams and squeals erupting from the crowd—Gratifying! For a moment, all was right in the world for Joe Salas.

As a parting shot, Lydia told him, as if an afterthought, "Mr. Salas, I got a phone call while you were entertaining our guests. Now what was it?" She put her finger trembling with anger to her lips while contemplating, "Your father. He's been in a car wreck. Now where did they say it was? On Bay Street somewhere." Her eyes glittered black and small in a thicket of mascara gloom. "Oh, and as you can probably guess—you're fired." She'd squeezed out a little rat-mouthed smile.

DIRTY BLOND HAIR tied into a graying weedy ponytail that recedes from a burnished bald spot on top, Joe Salas's reflection at forty-nine suggests a hard ridden sixty. Cycling past a scattering of derelict shops, he catches his fleeting specter in their dirty glass. Despite trying to turn away an anguished gaze, he's unable to resist the odd appalled sidelong glance at the face fluttering by—like his own, but grimacing, abased and mocking.

That biker, smudged and distorted, is not as he sees himself, despite the liberation of having just been fired from a job he hates. Him, forced to clean an art gallery amid other artists' work while his creative pastels, yellowed and torn, lie stuffed in the portfolio lashed to the back of his bicycle. He feels, after what just happened, empty—a lost, post-frenzy buzz he thought would've lasted at least till dark.

He races passed Magnolia Avenue, hot wind pushing at his back, inhaling the smell of Lake Eustis and creosote oozing from the railroad timbers snaking along its shores. He pedals and weaves through parked cars, skitters ahead of sluggish traffic, tailgates red light runners. Cycling feverishly, he imagines various horrible fates that could befall his ex-boss, Lydia Stein VonGloss, the arty broad he secretly calls the Botox Queen and pictures it in his mind a bloody stump where her head used to be.

Joe curses the traffic, speeds past Lakeview Avenue, over the sidewalk, and through the parking lot of the no-name filling station, gasoline vapors and burnt motor oil thick in the air. He's suddenly haunted by the memory of his Mom's death. Two years ago, to this day she'd left him and his father standing in a crowded hospital hallway as her body was wheeled past them to the freight elevator like so much dirty laundry, Joe's father holding her sweater as if she'd forgotten it. He and Joe, back at the house, had simply closed the door. It was all they could think to do.

Traffic is still moving, but slow. Joe thinks it's a good sign, no vehicles stopped in the roadway with impatient drivers when he pedals up the sidewalk. A crowd has gathered at the produce stand on Bay and Atwater, rubberneckers eager for gossip. Cantaloupes and oranges scattered across the lot collect in the gutter and splatter in the roadway. The air reeks with a cocktail of radiator fluid and juice fresh-squeezed under passing tires.

Three city patrol cars cluster in the parking lot, blue lights proclaiming a sideshow for those savoring gore. Other than the fruits, doesn't appear to be any. Joe recognizes his father's 1989 maroon Buick Century, only the rear trunk visible under the collapsed wooden produce stand, shredded chicken wire splayed across the back glass.

Watermelons lie busted and bleeding down the lot's incline. For an instant Joe sees it as blood, maybe his father's, imagines him crumpled underneath waiting for extraction. As he gets closer, he can just make out the driver's open door, the interior empty.

An ambulance idles behind the third patrol car, paramedics standing around as if there's nothing to do. Joe thinks maybe he's too late. He rides up behind the third patrol car and sees his father sitting in the passenger seat, the door wide open, holding a gauze pad to his forehead, walkin' stick between his knees. The air conditioner blows full blast in his face, his thin hair streaming back as if in a wind tunnel. The cop sitting behind the wheel writes on a clipboard, pulling at his sweaty life vest.

"Pop?" Joe asks.

Anthony Salas's eyes shift, his head moves only slightly.

Joe knows not to ask if he's all right. He's not. There's a look of embarrassed bewilderment in his father's eyes, that fix on Joe then turn away. Pop starts to speak, mouths a word in silence and stops.

"It's okay, Pop. I'll take care of it." Joe makes eye contact with the cop behind the wheel, nods, afraid of what the charge might be, not sure what to say or ask.

"You family?" the cop asks, still writing. He briefly glances up, notices the small leather bags suspended by chains on Joe's belt, places for personal stuff—money and mints. The leather gloves with the finger tips cut off make the cop shake his head at the oddball, remembers seeing the guy riding around town from time to time in the same khaki camp shirt and matching shorts like it's a uniform

"Son," Joe tells him, biting his thumb nail.

"What's your name?"

"Joe. Joseph Salas. What happened?"

Pop starts to speak, but tucks his chin in and goes silent again.

"Hit the gas instead of the brake. Lucky no one was hurt."

"My *father's* hurt."

"Refused treatment, Mr. Salas. Signed a waiver."

"Pop, why don't you let 'em look at you?" Joe reaches up to peek under the gauze. Pop yanks his head away and pushes off Joe's hand.

The cop nods as if Pop has confirmed his last statement, starts on the narrative for the report.

"Maybe the brakes are bad," Joe adds.

"We thought of that. Fire Rescue guys tested them. Work fine," the cop says, still writing. "Mr. Salas, are you aware of your father's driving history?"

"Why?"

"Did you know about the *five* other accidents this year?"

"Five?" Joe turns to the Buick tucked in by crushed fruit boxes.

The tow truck arrives with a beefy driver who's on a first name basis with everyone on scene. Kicks two by fours and split plywood aside to check underneath the Buick.

"A rise in accidents is a symptom of a bigger problem. I'm going to require him to take a test, Mr. Salas. I also recommend he visit his doctor, see if anything might be going on no one is aware of yet. I suspect his insurance will increase after this one, considering the damage. Does he live with you?"

"No, no he doesn't."

Joe leaves it at that, hopes the cop won't pry and ask why, say, 'You don't care for this old man?' Then he'll be forced to dig into the past, twenty years of crap neither he nor his dad would want to dredge up.

"Anything besides that bike to get around on?" The cop hands Pop the ticket for his signature. Pop peels the gauze from his head, his hand shaking, takes the pen and scribbles on the line. A two-inch gash smiles from his forehead. Blood dries at the edges and over the top of his right eye.

"Just my bike," Joe answers.

"Need to make arrangements to get him home then. His insurance has taken care of the rest. Looks like he'll need a replacement radiator."

Pop's Buick is hooked and dragged out of the produce stand. Remains of the store sign collapse onto the parking lot. Undamaged fruit disappears as gawkers drift off.

Joe walks around the car thinking of who to call, doesn't think the old man can manage on the back of his bike.

Broken grill pieces protrude from the Buick and a two by four impales the radiator. Dents in the hood, roof, and both front fenders. A wooden bench lies in splinters; the leg supports caught underneath the car frame dragging along unruly fruit that dislodges and makes a mad dash for the street.

It's drizzling when Joe's friend Betty shows up to take Pop home. Joe stands in the rain at the edge of the road and knows from this day forward his life will be changed. The cop told him as much in so many words.

2

dead fish

JOE HAS WANTED to be an artist for as long as he can remember. Being an artist allows him to escape into a world he creates and controls, to color it in the vibrant hues lacking in his real life, and to gesso it over if the final product doesn't meet his expectations. Living in canvas allows him to scream— silently. It shows in his work, emotionally dark behind vivid tropical colors that seem brazen lies, leaving the public with an uncomfortable sensation of foreboding. Critics call the work raw, too unorganized for commercial profit, mediocre at best.

Dusk, especially on the boardwalk by the lake, offers God's artwork. Joe watches the radiant sunset, warmed by a red orange wash against his pale skin, yet he is filled with an overwhelming depression that not even the soul-calming spectacle can assuage. Easy to resent it, envy the careless grandeur, regret the talent he lacks, mourn even more his lack of inspiration.

Over the railing, Joe watches a dead catfish float among the water lilies, pale, gutted. Water birds hover over it for a moment, pass on it leaving it for nibbling small fish. Joe wonders if, hooked by a fisherman, it was tossed aside because it didn't meet someone's expectations. Wonders if they'd considered the wastefulness, or reflected that fate had placed it, too, among living things.

Joe mounts his bike and pedals across Bay Street passing street tough locals on the sidewalk, careful not to look them in the eye. Uses peripheral vision to watch them until well out of reach. He's always sensed that he offends people. Not so much from his character, but from his elusive, introverted demeanor. As if they think he can't be trusted.

He leans his bike against the brick wall in an empty alley and collects discarded paper and cardboard boxes out of a commercial dumpster and piles them on the crud-encrusted asphalt. He retrieves his tattered work from the portfolio, lays them on the pile, lights a match, and flips it on top. The edges curl and smoke, orange red, eating away. Ash flakes blacken the air, drift to the rooflines.

Mourning the loss of his final sketch and the end of a promised art career from Lydia, Joe notices, even now, the way the colors play off each other. But like the work, the promise evaporates, replaced with bad news and no severance pay.

Six minutes destroys the work. Chunks of cooling ash disintegrate under his foot; smoke fills his lungs. The portfolio hangs gaping from his bike as if in the throes of its own silent scream.

3

shaving prunes

ANTHONY "POP" SALAS' place is in the Eustis city limits, a modest cement block home built in the 1950s, surrounded by newer homes feverishly constructed within the last ten years in a mixed neighborhood. Turned out a flood of tourists didn't want to leave.

Homes are clustered together; Pop's is on a cul-de-sac, his backyard fenced in with chain link, the far end dumping into natural wooded acreage with an artesian pond.

A lone dead pine towers above the tree line like a giant skeletonized scarecrow stripped of clothing.

Pop likes the view, feels the developers don't know about it yet, but knows it's a matter of time before bulldozers level the land and build half-million-dollar estate homes four to an acre. Any hole filled with water is deemed lakefront, even if nothing more than an overrated retention pond.

For now, Pop has an unobstructed view of natural Florida, its subtle seasons and the varied wildlife that call it home.

At eighty, Pop starts his day at five sharp, never sleeps in, never travels, and never wants to be a bother. It takes longer now to dress himself. Arthritis seizes the joints under thin sun spotted skin draping his frail bones. He bends now slightly at the waist and shoulders. Movement's slow, pain gauged by the failing ability to shuffle his bad right hip, stiff from a Korean war shrapnel wound. Friendly fire. Some days are better than others. Rainy days just miserable.

Despite these physical ailments, his tongue is opinionated and often, sharp. At times, cantankerous. He's relinquished his freedom to the Florida Department of Motor Vehicles with little fight. Nothing more than a muttered argument he didn't want them to hear anyway.

Simply not lifting his leg to the brake had caused the accident. The muscle rebelled, froze, and he'd stared in horror as the Buick rolled onward. At the last minute, the spasm subsided, and in panic, he'd jammed his foot on the accelerator instead of the brake. *Damn!* Citizens were glad to force one more geezer off the streets, didn't care that he quietly mourned this final vestige of independence.

Days after the accident, in front of the mirror above the bureau, Pop tightens his leather belt, his left hand shaking from the ebb and flow of a tremor, a neurological problem, the prodrome of dementia. He pulls his false teeth out of the soaking glass, squirts on Denture Grip and sticks them in his mouth. Smacks his lips at his reflection. Minty fresh.

He brilliantines the small cowlick of hair that mutinies to a spike—a chronic scrimmage for the better part of seventy years—then pulls the dry bloody gauze off his forehead and inspects the head wound in the mirror. Seen worse. Goes into the bathroom, fashions a half-assed bandage out of toilet paper and sticks it on with Scotch Tape. Decides to skip the shave today. Pulls the sheet over the pillow and limps to the kitchen in his ratty slippers.

Fog drifts across the back yard, hovering just above the tops of the newly planted ligustrum hedges along the chain link to the shed at the corner, a scene from the kitchen window Pop looks forward to every morning. Most mornings the view is clear, but when the dew point is just right, moisture collects like a soft blanket shrouding all things beyond the walls.

He fills the thirty-year-old percolator with water from the tap, spoons in a chicory blend, and plugs it in. Taking two cups from the cabinet, he places them on the kitchen table along with a box of bran cereal, a half-gallon of skim milk, jar of prunes, and the Daily Herald. Takes his time getting into the chair.

Joe slithers in, hung over, eyes half shut.

"Jo Jo. Got coffee goin' there." Pop makes a stiff half turn as if the coffee pot will heave itself from the counter to the table. Freezes with his hand outstretched.

Joe waits, expecting Pop to say something else. "How's your head there?"

"Not so bad." Pop turns back to his cereal bowl and begins to eat. He unfolds the paper, section at a time, shaking his head now and then as if another truth has been confirmed in the editorial. Eyes to the paper he asks, "How'd you sleep?"

"You live with that dog long?"

Pop looks up, confused.

Joe rubs crust from his eyes, "Damn thing yapped all night."

"Dee Dee, the big black girl next door. Her dog. Hear it more in the room you're in. Advantages to a hearing aid. Sometimes turn it off at night. Don't hear a damn thing."

"I hear just fine."

"Yeah, betcha do. I'll talk to her, but don't expect much. Not a friendly sort, that one. Give her lot of room. Why I put that big wood fence up on the side she's on." Pop crawls out of the chair, goes to the pot, and pours coffee into his cup. The cup clatters on the saucer as he carries it back to the table.

"Lived here long, the Dee Dee woman?" Joe pours a cup, the aroma taking him back decades in this very room.

"Year or so. Bought from old Elsie, remember her? Mom looked in on her every day. Had to go into a nursing home, no one to care for her after Mom passed. Dee Dee woman said the poor old thing left the place a mess. Lots of cats. Garbage and stuff stuck around like scabs. Want cereal?" Pop slurps milk from the spoon. A limp bran flake hangs from the stubble on his chin.

"No, not hungry."

"That woman kick you out?"

Pop pushes the bowl away and starts on the prunes—sees the obvious disgust in Joe's face.

"Not my favorite either. Eat 'em last."

"What woman?"

Pop screws up his face, stabs a prune. "Where you work!" Bites off half and prune juice trickles from the corner of his mouth. "Where you goin' next? Jobs hard to find around here. You can forget that drawin' crap and find a real job."

A severed prune quivers on the fork.

"It is a real job. It was."

"Whatcha do to get canned?"

"Bad customer relations."

"Yeah?"

"I'll find something. Shop says the car will be done in a day or so," Joe says to change the subject. Stares out the kitchen window.

Movement through the fading mist along the edge of the pond catches his eye. A turkey vulture drifts in from out of the mist and lands at the pond's grassy rim. He can see two of them now, black, stoic. Within seconds, a third one circles the dead pine and lands on the broken stumps at the top.

"Big birds," Joe mumbles.

"What's that?"

Louder, Joe says, "The birds out there. Like they're gathering for a meetin'."

"What's that?"

Pop turns stiffly in his chair and adjusts the hearing aid. Sees that whatever it is has Joe's full attention. "Get all kinds. Not as many song birds as before. Not since that Dee Dee woman. Her dog chases 'em off. Not so many now."

"You ever see the big ones down there, the vultures?"

"Them? Been comin' round for years. Don't bother anyone. Big story in the paper … last month I think. Roostin' on folk's houses, pool screens, shittin' on everything. They say their shit's like acid. Protected, the paper said. Can't kill 'em."

"You don't say?"

"Yeah. That's what it said."

Pop gets up, places the coffee cup in the bowl and sets them in the sink. "Listen here JoJo, since you're out of work and all, you can stay here 'till you get on your feet. Whenever you feel like it." He squeezes dish soap in the rag and holds it under the faucet. The silence is long and awkward— Joe staring out the window and Pop washing dishes.

"I'll leave the pot. Get more coffee there when you want."

Joe nods.

"You can even move those boxes in the room you're in to the shed out there. Give you more space."

"What's in 'em?" Joe asks eyes still fixed on the window.

"Old crap. Just things I've been packin' up. Too damn lazy to take it out. Do what you want. It's all the same to me."

A slight half turn, Joe starts another question, stops, lets it drop.

13

4

predisposition

"*RAISIN PIE. IN* the army, that's all you got. Little squares. They didn't rot, you see. They'd come dried and stuck in boxes for months, but when we got 'em, they'd be gone in minutes." Pop points a finger at the windshield, "If stored too long they'd get brick hard. You could break a tooth." Taps the dash with a knuckle.

He stops talking, watches things out the window go by as the car moves through town, and suddenly as if he'd just remembered the rest of the story says, "But, it was better than sucking glue off paper." Pop's tongue rolls across his top denture. "Damned sticky things they were, too, raisin pie. Jammed in your teeth and we couldn't brush. Not so much. Teeth'ed rot and get infected.

"Sittin' in that damn foxhole, I seen other fellas do it, you know, take the bayonet off their rifle, jam it in the mouth, crack, pop, and out it come. Old rotten tooth. Good riddance. Some fellas passed out. We'd stick his bayonet back on his rifle and prop him up. Eventually he'd come to. Then another box of raisin pie'ed come along and be gone quick like the last. It was a helluva thing. Don't like raisins much. Be okay to eat 'em now though 'cause I ain't got any teeth left." Pop clicks his dentures together.

Joe issues a grunt just to let Pop know he's listening. Sort of. He's heard the raisin pie story before, can recite it. When his Mom was alive, she'd interrupt Pop's endless storytelling by asking a question and it always stopped him cold. Apparently early in their relationship she had discovered that little trick, but now that she's gone it just seems disrespectful to use it on him like that.

So, Joe nods, mumbles a yes now and then, thinking of anything but the army or raisin pie.

"You drive better. Remember when I took you out that first time and you, you were comin' to that light and it turned yella? You panicked and were gonna' brake but hit the gas instead? Flew through that intersection doin' about forty, up on the shoulder and down the ditch we went."

Pop's thin lips peel around his false teeth.

"Predisposition," Joe says pulling into the Walgreen's. "Mom gave me lessons after that. Don't remember you laughing about it then."

"Yeah, well ..." Pop drifts off, hands over a prescription. "Damn funny now."

"ANYWHERE ELSE?" Joe asks crawling back into the car.

"Publix might be good. Gettin' low on grub." Pop takes the bag from Joe's hand and opens it, takes out the brown prescription bottle and pulls it close to his eyes. "This the right stuff?"

"It's the right stuff, Pop."

"They can mix it up on you, you know. Give you the wrong stuff or too much. Call it a clerical error. Next thing you know you're face down in the toilet. Happened to Verge. Remember Verge?"

Joe works his way through the crowded parking lot. "Not really, Pop. It's the right stuff."

"They mixed it up on him and he starts shakin' and gaggin', floppin' around like a fish and down he goes."

Pop takes the lid off and picks out a pill, holds it up to his face.

"He die?" Joe asks.

"Naw, a few days in the hospital's all. Killed on I-95," Pop says dropping the pill back in the bottle.

"Because of the meds?"

"Car flew across the median. Hit him head-on."

"Sorry to hear that."

"He was an asshole. Insisted we all call him *Colonel*. I think he was just a lieutenant colonel. Can't prove it," Pop stares out the window. "Don't suppose it matters now."

"Don't suppose it does."

Pop leans into the windshield, "Get that space."

"What space? Crowded here. Should a gone to the new one by Beall's."

"She's comin' out, just wait."

"We're blocking traffic, Pop. Pissin' people off."

"Horse shit, just wait."

Horns start to beep behind them. Pop cusses an old lady out as if she can hear him. On the fourth horn beep Pop starts to open the door, gripping his walkin' stick like a weapon.

Joe knows he's going to step out and start yelling profanities to no one in particular, just anyone in the line of fire. To his relief the old lady pulls away and he tucks the car into the slot without further incident. It brings back memories of Pop swearing at traffic, or at neighbors he felt had wronged him in some trivial way. The embarrassment feels the same, the heat on the back of his neck, sweaty palms, knot in the gut.

"Tried to hit on her," Pop announces as he pushes the door shut and steps into the lane blocking traffic again. Joe grabs his arm and ushers him closer to the rear of parked cars, forcing him to a stop before they cross in front of the Publix grocery.

"Who hit on her?"

"Verge. Mom told me about it."

"When that happen?"

"After he died." Pop grabs a shopping cart, throws his walkin' stick in, and shoves the cart through the store as if he doesn't care who's in the way.

"He hit on her after he died?"

"No, *Who-Ass*. She told me about it after he died! Damn good thing. I'd a sent him home to glory early."

Joe stands at the dairy counter, stunned. Pop hasn't called him *Who-Ass* in thirty years.

POP SITS IN his recliner reliving his war days, watching John Wayne blowing Japs out of bunkers on the Afternoon Theater.

Joe wanders from room to room, ghosts introduce themselves, memories blossom that he has been comfortable to let die on the vine.

Pop's bedroom is exactly as it was two years ago. The same bedspread, same knickknacks peppered on the bedside tables, faint smell of menthol rub and Dial soap.

There's a collection of containers on the bureau, some he can remember giving his Mom throughout the years. Cut glass perfume bottles, a hand carved wooden box he made in middle school—still filled with small jewelry. The tissue box, the prescription bottle for cholesterol, the brush and comb set handed down from her mother. All coated with a film of fine dust.

He picks up her perfume bottle and inhales, runs his fingers across the brush imbedded with strands of silver hair. He sets the bottle back and pulls open the top drawer where her clothing waits for her return, as do the clothes on her side of the closet, and the winter things stored under the bed.

Two years she's been gone, but her things still wait.

In the bathroom, Joe finds her Skin-so-Soft bath oil, her toothbrush in the holder next to Pop's, her half empty tube of toothpaste. She'd told him once that if you wanted to get along in a relationship, each should keep separate toothpaste. It was Crest for her, Colgate for him. "It keeps the peace," she'd said.

Joe's chest tightens, fills with pain, the things waiting, him waiting. Pride kept him from saying words while she was alive, words she needed to hear, words that would have made a difference. He tells her now from time to time in his head as if she might possess some supernatural power to hear his thoughts, wonders what she would have said.

It occurs to him what Pop's life must be like living here without her, waiting, passing the time, leading a half-life. Merely existing until together again. A daily routine with no passion, memories held so close they've become his life, not interested in new memories, the old ones sacrosanct, not to be defiled by actual living.

Joe sits on the edge of the bathtub and realizes Pop has never once complained, never uttered a bitter word about his loneliness. He must feel it, because just sitting among her things, Joe feels lonely. He feels lonely for Pop in a deep, painful way, as an outsider, an intruder to their sixty-three years of secret life. He senses the whole house has become hallowed ground and it's he who's unclean.

5

malathion cocktail

THREE IN THE morning is a sacred hour. Not to the damned dog. It yaps at shadows, at possums that wander up from the pond hopeful for garbage or left out scraps then goes silent just long enough to allow Joe to fall back asleep. Starts yappin' again as if it knows.

The barking incites dreams of his Mom, times and conversations he doesn't consciously remember, places he's never been, with vague silhouettes always watching, judging, whispering—

"This Atwater? Thought I was on Bay Street, but looking for Atwater. Jeez, I think I'm lost." One way left, one way right, a siren in the distance. Joe's Mom insisting, "Go on, Joe, you gotta find him."

Lost his bike. Thought he was on it. He stands now in the middle of Bay Street under the school zone sign, yellow lights turn red, the siren getting louder, Joe hears his Mom yell, "You gotta find him, Joe. I think he's hurt bad!"

Heart pounding, sweaty palms, Joe sees a guy standing in the medium holding a 'will work for food' sign. "You seen my Pop? He's been in a car crash. Atwater, they said. Can't find it."

"Moved Atwater," Beggar says holding his sign. No one on the street. Not a soul.

"How can they move a street?"

"Dropped it at the end of Kurt Street. More room for the fruit."

"That's right!" Joe yells. Suddenly remembers Pop's Buick plowed into a fruit stand. What he was told. "How far?"

"Can't help you now. Gotta get these kids across the street."

"What kids? They're no damn kids. How do I get to Atwater?"

"Take the train."

"What train? It that far? Told me he was just down the street. Could get there on my bike!"

"Don't see no bike. Need help across the street?" Beggar asks, points towards the sound of an on-coming train with an orange in his hand. "Better go quick. You miss it, he's dead!"

With each new awakening Joe's re-immersion in sleep brings more frightening dreams, so by the first light of day they've burgeoned into sharp-edged nightmares.

Pop doesn't say much at breakfast, senses the dark mood Joe's brought to the table. After a few days of living together, a routine has developed. Joe has assimilated into Pop's world, given up much of his own. Without work or art, he doesn't have much.

"Goin' to Wal-Mart in a little, Pop."

"Yeah? Whatcha gettin'?"

"Plastic containers. Thought I'd transfer the stuff from those old cardboard boxes into plastic ones. You know, the ones with the lock lids?"

"Yeah? Maybe you can buy you some new clothes while you're at it."

"What's wrong with these?"

"That all you got?"

"No, but I like these."

"Looks like you're going on safari. And what do you keep in the little pussy bags there?"

"Stuff is all. It bother you that much?"

"Yeah, sorta does. But do whatcha want."

"Come along if you want. Leavin' soon."

Pop nods, throws his hand up as if to brush him out of the house. "Stories comin' on. You go."

Joe stands by the door watching the old man without his realizing he's still there, watches him take the remote, pull it to his face, stick his thumb on the channel button, then point it at the TV.

The Guiding Light. Pop's favorite. His Mom got the old man hooked on it after he retired from the insurance company. They'd talk about the characters as if they lived in the neighborhood, Pop remarking how much of a slut Reva was and how Josh could do better, Mom saying how Reva was misunderstood which launched into an afternoon of who was in denial and who was better off. Joe smiles.

At the car, Joe sees the Dee Dee woman collecting her paper, the yappy dog at her heel. Not as small as it sounds through the fence, mid-sized Chow mix, black fur, lots of needle-sharp teeth. Bares them at him behind her back. The shrill yap seems to him to be caused by neutering, no more male hormones, just bitterness.

Dee Dee's unfriendly, doesn't engage in neighborly conversation. Almost as if she knows he hates her damned dog, can smell it on him.

Joe takes it all in, she in the muu muu housecoat wide open from the breast down, pedal pushers so tight her brown thighs rupture the seams, gut puddled around the waist band.

The sight antagonizes him. "You let that dog out all night? Why don't you keep him in? Yaps and howls all night. No one can sleep."

No comment from her end, just suspicion. She screws up her face, her thick lips pursed like a medieval gargoyle. At least in his mind.

He shudders as he backs out of the driveway, can feel her eyes on him until he's safely out of sight.

THE SHED, WEATHERED but with good bones, the lumber pressure treated, not the warped four by fours thrown on the discount pile back of the lumber yard. Not in this shed. Twenty years ago, Pop took great care to craft this project, hand-selecting each board, sighting to see if it was true, checking it for fractures and knotholes. More than a shed, it's a warehouse harboring the Salas' dying lives.

Spider webs hang thick across the shed door, a month-to-month rental turned yearly sub-lease. Eight-legged tenants sucking the life from unsuspecting insect visitors. Even tearing the anchor lines from the webs doesn't faze them, and not until the web shrinks away do they defiantly move on. Joe shakes the lock, coaxing the key into the rusted channel.

Mildew and used motor oil stench fill his nose in total darkness. He flips on the light with his elbow, sees there's nowhere to set the box and drops it at his feet. Joe can see the shed needs reorganization, a hardy pitch session for decades' worth of accumulated crap.

Partially decomposed cardboard boxes stacked to his left absorb spilled Havoline forty-weight motor oil and a half empty bottle of Malathion that makes the room reek. It seems to affect insects seeking cover in the dark—dead cockroaches on their backs, legs tucked in, silverfish, centipedes—all waiting for Mr. Shop Vac.

He finds a wooden footlocker, army green, faded shipping addresses stenciled across the lid stored under the workbench, no lock, no interest in years. Pop doesn't come in here much anymore. Too much stuff overwhelms the room. Open the door, find a spot, shove stuff in, close the door quick. Who cares what lives in there? Whoever it is can eat the shit up, just don't show itself.

Joe's history, too, is dying in here. Neglected battered toys, games with missing pieces, the baseball equipment Pop bought *hoping*—another painful reminder of failure and disappointment covered in gray mold.

Sports wasn't in Joe no matter how hard Pop tried to convince him otherwise. He wanted to draw, hated the running, sliding, pain. The ball slamming into his glove hurt his hand. And when the pitcher landed a fast ball in Joe's gut that was the last straw. After that, he refused to touch a ball of any kind, ever.

Pop didn't speak to him for days—called him "pussy boy." His mom ended that, told Pop to keep his name-calling to himself. The term *Who-Ass* was coined soon after. *Shit head* was ruled out. Had to call him something. *Joe* just didn't seem appropriate for the way he felt about the kid, needed to let him know where he stood. At first Joe didn't understand what *Who-Ass* meant, but soon just the tone and the way it was said let him know it was derogatory. Not a joke slap on the back and laugh sort of thing. It was used to remind him of his failings, the stupid *Who-Ass* label as if tattooed on his forehead—just in case he wasn't sure.

A Rat scurries under the workbench thumping and knocking paint cans together. Joe thinks he remembers seeing a rat trap under the kitchen sink.

After a good three hours, black trash bags pile up on the curb, filled with empty spray cans, split water hose, broken tire gauge, moldy clothes, ancient Christmas decorations, and an assortment of the mercifully unidentifiable.

One very large rat is stuck to a yellow sticky trap bought at the Winn Dixie, eyes glazed over, bloody foot half eaten off.

The cleanout leaves the shed with a nice open space, the bench empty, waiting for a project, the cutting tools arranged on pegboard above it, pruning saws, loppers, shears, and a surprisingly sharp machete. Screwdrivers find a home in the toolbox underneath and there's even a nice utility sink to wash up after. That seems to be where the rat lived, its nest compiled from scraps of fabric, fiberglass insulation, and dried leaves from Pop's garden. Now dumped on top of the corpse.

Across the yard, Joe drags the last garbage bag, the one that holds most of his childhood toys, grade school diplomas, report cards, certificates of award from elementary school. God knows why his Mom kept those. Every kid got one. He was nothing special. And early drawings—she'd appreciated them. Seemed to at the time.

A shadow the size of a small plane passes over the yard. Joe ducks, looks up as a turkey vulture sweeps just over the tree line, flaps its wings to gain altitude and makes another swing over the house.

Stepping from the side yard to the front, Joe is startled by two vultures less than twenty feet from where he's standing. The bag in his hand drops at his feet. Can't concentrate and hold on to it. Two vultures fight over the contents of an open garbage bag at the curb.

One vulture pulls something away from the bag and hops across the sidewalk with it. From where Joe stands, it appears to be the rat still stuck to the yellow sticky pad, black feathers now added to it. The second vulture hops after the first, a flurry of black feathers, hissing, aggravated, pissing on the sidewalk. The rat is severed, only the top half still attached to the adhesive pad.

Dee Dee's front door opens and her dog flies out in a whirl of black fur, teeth, and spit. Dee Dee clutches the doorframe, screaming in a voice that rivals the dog's, bolts from the porch, hair curlers flying, fat rolls undulating, losing a pink mule on the top step. Stops dead the moment she realizes she's way too close to the action. It's the first time she's ever been struck speechless.

Vulture One takes to the air having swallowed its half of the spoils, wingspread stretching from what seems one side of the road to the other, barely clearing the body shop on the next street over.

Dee Dee Dog makes contact with the second bird just below the right wing, vulnerable, the sticky pad stuck on its bill, but now forced to defend itself. With a leap, it spins and becomes all outstretched wings, backing up, hissing, and in one fluid motion, pukes the remains of road kill eaten off Orange Avenue.

Dee Dee Dog stops barking, stops growling, inspects the regurgitated gift leaving just enough time for Vulture Two to take flight, sticky pad and all.

Dee Dee swings around at Joe, coiled hair spiking straight up, one curler still attached and hanging over her right eye. She glances down at the dog, sweeps it up in her arms and stumbles back into the house.

ON A PILING near shore, a great blue heron perches motionless in silhouette like a fugitive lawn ornament.

Three or four people fish at the edge of the boardwalk, bait buckets at their feet, poles over the calm water, concrete walkway stained with fish blood.

Tourists stroll around taking in the view and then get reeled in by wisps of charbroiled smoke from the shore's Gator's restaurant.

Joe hops off his bike and leans it against the railing. Betty stands in her usual spot with a fishing pole in her hands, two more poles attached to the railing with clamps, line slackened by floating bobbers. Three small fish swim in the bucket. Almost enough for a meal.

He can always spot her, cigarette hanging from the side of her mouth, squinting from the smoke's sting. Hard looking for someone in her late forties, trauma in her eyes, experiences that can't be buried deep enough. Hispanic women, he thinks, should age better than that, but not her. Skin's like leather. Ten or twenty years from now she'll be laid up in an ICU hooked to a respirator praying to die. That's what he said to convince her to stop smoking, alarmed by the change in her looks in just the past year.

Two years in state prison didn't help her looks none, either. Cancer maybe. Doesn't bring it up, wouldn't want to scare her with the suggestion of it. He'd noticed the cough. She smokes as if it's salvation and drinks to smooth the edges. Joe doesn't mind the drinking part. To stop her means so would he. He's lightened up on the smoking issue. It pisses her off every time he brings it up, and lately it's gotten between them. For him … stopping …well, giving up one more thing important in his life is out of the question.

He stands unnoticed watching her pile her lifeless hennaed hair on top of her head and secure it with a hair clip. A style she's worn since high school.

The pole tugs at the railing bringing a moderately cheap thrill. Betty reels fast before a bigger fish eats her catch. The blue heron tilts its head, eyeing with interest as Betty pulls the line out of the water and clutches a sad flat excuse of a fish, gasping, resigned.

"What you got?" Joe leans over and looks in the bucket.

"What do they look like?"

"Ugly. Should you be eatin' those?"

"Crappies."

"Then why eat 'em if they taste crappy?"

"They're called CRAPPIES! Don't taste crappy."

"Fine, eat what you want. Don't know why you can't buy 'em from the store."

"They're *free.* And I always eat. Didn't anyone ever tell you it's impolite to look in someone's bucket?"

Joe leans on the railing, staring into the water. His reflection ripples on the surface. "You just made that up."

"No, I didn't. Old fisherman's rule. Keep your nose out of another's bucket. How's Pop?" Betty unhooks the fish and drops it in the bucket. She squints at Joe to catch him in a lie.

"Better. Doesn't say much."

"They take his license?"

"Yeah. They won't give it back," Joe says gazing in the water.

"How's he getting around?"

"I take him."

Betty wipes her fish hands on her black spandex shorts and bends over to collect the tackle box, her breasts just shy of falling out of the blue print halter-top, the left nipple playing peek-a-boo.

A tattoo stands out on her fleshy right shoulder, a rose with a single drop of blood falling from the petal, the name "*Jamie*" beneath. Prison ink tattoos on each knuckle, love on one hand, hate on the other. Joe thinks they're cool. He shares a similar single life, on the edge—familiar failures, never a success. He tries not to stare at the peek-a-boo nipple. Does anyway.

"You're takin' care of him? How'd that happen?" she asks shaking her head. "Man, can't see that happening for the long haul. Few weeks you'll kill each other."

"He needs me. No one to help him out now. Gettin' old, Betty."

Gathering the poles, Betty steps into her green Dollar Store flip-flops, "Who? You or him?"

"Lonely I think, with Mom gone. Hasn't changed a damn thing in two years."

"What, you mean the house?"

Joe picks up the bucket of fish and walks off the boardwalk with Betty on his heels. "I mean it's like she never died. All her stuff in the house, her clothes, personal stuff like that. Even the damn toothbrush."

"Well, he doesn't want to let her go."

"Never will from what I see."

Betty stops, gives him an all too familiar expression that says he's a dumb-ass and should know it. "No, don't think he will. Some losses never fade." Betty's trauma swells to the surface as if a memory's replaying in vivid color.

He can't look at her. He's sorry he's wiped her nose in it again. "I get that. It must make it worse having the stuff layin' around like that, always reminding him. I'm not criticizing," Joe says.

"Maybe for him it's comfort. Eases the loneliness. Memories are all we're left with in the end anyway." Betty says it with a PhD on the subject of memories.

Joe hands her the bucket and pulls the bike away from the railing. Coming here's a bad idea, putting this in front of her. Him forgetting. "Sorry I brought it up."

"Ricky's probation officer came by today," she says adjusting her top.

Stopping his momentum, Joe says, "What he want?"

"Paroling him out. Wanted to give me a heads up."

"He comin' back here, you think?" He can see it scares her.

She shrugs, afraid to explore the possibilities. "What about your art, Joe?"

"What?"

Betty collects her gear, checks the fish in the bucket, debating on whether to take them home after all. "You gonna take the art somewhere else?"

"Don't want to talk about it. Folks want the stick figures in primary colors. Artistically, I'm a dinosaur. Not that important anymore."

"Bullshit my friend," she says. "That's been your dream since ninth grade."

"Not workin' out. Like everything else."

"Stop the pity party. You got the talent. No one can take it away."

"Anyway, I gotta take Pop up to the VA hospital tomorrow. Catch you later, Betty girl."

Joe pauses for traffic at the edge of the road, crosses Bay and disappears behind Badcock's furniture store.

Betty stands with the bucket in her hand, watching intently until he disappears. Maybe she should tell him the secret she's been keeping all these years. And that makes her think of Ricky who's coming home. Better not tell. Not yet.

6

palm spikes

STERILE WHITE BLOCK walls, polished tile, utility fixtures, not homey, not decorated, metal chairs in the waiting room, no magazines. No smoking, no singing, no loud talking, cough in your sleeve, please.

Three doors down, Pop lies in a ward shared with three other vets, all in various stages of dying. Pop calls it the dying room. He meets guys here at the VA while waiting for tests and never sees them again. Joe can't convince him they've moved on, gotten better, didn't need the room anymore.

"You always need the room. Once you check in, it's a matter of time before they take you to the basement," Pop warns.

"Are no basements," Joe tells him.

"Somewhere in this building they take your dead ass to a cold room and that's where you're processed. Like Soylent Green."

"Soylent Green?"

"That seventies Charleston Heston movie. Starvin' over-populated world. Folks volunteer to watch a movie of what nature used to be like before it was wiped out, then get shipped off. Edward G. Robinson's in it. You remember. Society forced to eat little green squares of human processin'."

"They don't process the dead, Pop. They don't eat 'em, either."

"Then, where are they? In Spam cans or little green squares," Pop says.

"They're just out, livin' on the golf course, gettin' jiggy at the retirement home. I don't know pop, quit thinkin' the worst."

"Yeah, well, sit your ass in here long enough and just wait. You'll find out. Just wait. Don't the Hawaiians got an appetite for Spam?"

Exasperated, Joe shuts up, knows the fight will raise Pop's blood pressure and keep him here longer. Each time Pop needs tests it becomes more and more difficult to get him to go. Each time he does, he seems frailer, more frightened. When pinned down for a reason, he evades and shuts down. Come to think of it, the old dude by the door never did come back after his test. Joe keeps it to himself, gets up and points at the TV. "Got the clicker there. Goin' down stairs for a coffee. Get you one?"

Pop waves him off. "You go."

Joe holds his palm up, glad to go despite the guilt of leaving the old man alone. Wonders how he gets along, what goes on in his head.

Pop takes count of his mates, the room silent other than the constant beeping of patients' monitors. Seventy-year-old Ted Something from Ohio is next to the window, shoved full of tubes, plastic bags hanging on both sides dripping into his veins. Pop thinks the old guy needs more than tests. Looks like he's dying. Wonders if they've shown the old dude the *Movie* yet.

He has weird thoughts like, do people from other states taste different—if you had to eat one?

Sammy across the room has dementia, asks the same damn question over and over ever since he checked in, "Who are you?" After the first half hour of answering, Pop just clams up. And it seems Sammy just forgets anyone's there and falls asleep. None of them ever have visitors, makes the whole thing worse.

Pop takes the remote and switches on the TV, surfs the channels at random. Suddenly fear grips him like a great bird of prey, followed by loneliness so deep that death has no ransom over him.

Joe's been gone too long, maybe gotten nosey and stumbled in on the *"processing"* and become part of tomorrow's lunch special. Pop stews in anxiety until Joe finally walks through the door with his paper cup, and Pop hits the channel button pretending to be interested in whatever is on the screen.

"Whatcha watchin' Pop?" Joe sets the coffee on Pop's tray, pulls a chair closer to the bed and sits down.

"Nothin' much."

"When did you start watchin' TV preachers?"

"Benny Hinn," Pop says, relieved he can remember the name after all this time. Mom would watch, suckin' air when people fell out on the floor, awed at such profound wonders.

"Gave someone a palm spike to the forehead," he tells Joe. "This guy here, some sort of brain thing goin' on. Palm spiked him so hard I think he knocked the guy out!"

"Thought that was supposed to be the Holy Spirit workin'?" Joe ventures.

Pop shakes his head and waves the remote in the air, "Naw, knocked him out cold. He'll come to in a minute and old

Benny'll tell him he's cured, the headache's from the power of the Lord. Hallelujah. You watch."

Joe takes the remote out of his hand and surfs through a half-dozen channels, settling on a basketball game. Sammy groans from across the room and yells, "Get that pussy moving!" and goes silent again.

They both watch him. "Dude's not right in the head, is he?" Joe says it more as a statement, doesn't expect Pop to give an answer or know what the old guy's screaming about.

"Maybe, but sounds like he's in a good place."

The TV audience erupts in jeers and moans. A player limps off the court with the help of teammates. Pop shakes his head in disgust.

"Pussies. Fall down and get up cryin' like little girls. No real men anymore. In my day he'd a got up, slapped that knee back in place and gone on. Maybe old Sammy's hearin' the game."

Joe throws the cup in the trash. "Don't think he can see it from where he's at, Pop."

"I don't think so either. A different pussy, I guess." Pop points to the TV screen, "I bet if they had the same rules for basketball players as they do for racehorses there'd be damned fewer injuries, tell you what."

"Why's that, Pop?"

"If a player got too many injuries, they'd just take him out and shoot him! After a few of those, you'd see the rest of 'em out there hobbling around on their casts, playing, broken leg and all."

The nurse comes in and sets a lunch tray on Pop's wheelie table. She checks his chart and takes his pulse. Her hands are cold. Dead hands, Pop thinks. Doesn't remember the dead coming back in the *Movie.*

"… your lunch?" she asks. Pop doesn't hear the first part of the question. Invents his own. Something along the lines of 'did he want Florida or Wisconsin Spam added to his lunch?' and he mumbles something to the effect he can still afford real meat. She takes off the stainless-steel cover and sets it aside. Some unidentifiable meat covered in pale gravy, mashed potatoes and wilted green beans. He doesn't realize he's made a comment about the food, how he can't be sure what it really is.

"It has seven vitamins and minerals," she says. That's what Pop thinks she said.

"You can get that in a good bag of dog food," he tells her.

She pauses a moment confused, "Your doctor will be in later and give you instructions for your medications. He'll sign your release papers so you can leave this afternoon. How's that sound?"

Pop looks around her at Sammy, the constant blip of his monitor the only sign he's still alive. Ted Something rolls onto his side and starts snoring. Pop thinks they aren't far gone enough yet, thinks he remembers you had to be on the edge of death before you got to see the *Movie.*

"Sooner the better," he mumbles.

THE WEATHER'S TURNED, gray clouds racing ahead of a storm front, eating sky in an ominous threat. Joe's on the sofa, a roll of cheap paper towels tucked in the crook of his arm with seven or eight waded-up sheets littering the coffee table.

It's a head cold, snot invasion of the sinus with a high school band marching behind the eyes. He's not moved in two hours, embraced self-pity like a favorite stuffed toy. Channels on the TV skitter by every few seconds because he's bored, nudging despondency, the remote sweating in his hand. Sighs, thinks he has a fever. Coughs and gags into another paper towel and throws it at the others. Figures maybe pneumonia.

Hangs his head off the sofa so snot can drain freely into yet another paper towel.

"Makin' lunch. Feel like lunch, JoJo?" Pop stands in the dining room, his neck stretched out like a turtle trying to leave the shell.

Joe doesn't look up. Pulls himself upright on the sofa, suffering. "Do whatcha want. All the same to me."

Pop turns for the kitchen.

"Got a cold from that place," Joe calls out.

Pop stops, makes an uncommitted half turn, "Got a cold you say?"

"Yeah, from the place there. Lots of germs. Think I caught somethin'."

"Be glad that's all you got. Like I said, folks disappear in there," Pop says limping back to the kitchen.

"Christ, it's a cold. Not cancer," Joe mutters.

The remote settles on a program from a cable home and garden show called "The Modern Pros." It's not a conscious choice, no real choice at all. It's simply the last channel squeezed from the remote.

Some guy in a Hawaiian shirt stands in front of a large table with a fish on it, gills moving, eyes desperate, not unlike those Betty pulls off her hooks. *Gyotaku*, he says, a Japanese word meaning fish impression, an ancient art form, art being the one word that catches Joe's attention. It makes him sit upright and forget his cold. He watches intrigued, hoping for a morsel that will launch his defunct career.

By the time the segment ends, he's scalped five sheets of paper towels from the roll and filled them with pen-written notes. It's the first time in weeks that anything ignites a spark in Joe Salas.

Smoke drifts in from the kitchen. Something burning.

As Joe drags himself off the sofa, the smoke alarm begins screaming in the dining room. Pop comes out of the kitchen waving a dish towel, limps around in a circle, stops, throws his hands in the air and bellows, *"Shit!"*

"Whatcha doin', Pop?" Joe looks past him at smoke boiling into the dining room. Yanking the towel from Pop's hand and slapping it over his own mouth he disappears into the kitchen.

"Just a little smoke is all," Pop calls behind him, "No worry."

Grilled cheese sandwiches. Not quite to the point of bursting into flame. Lots of smoke. Two of them sit in the skillet, crusted black, smoke billowing exuberantly around each.

Joe grabs a potholder, grabs the skillet by the handle and throws it, sandwiches and all, in the sink. He turns on the faucet, water sizzling and popping from the heat, smoke alarm relentless.

Pop sticks his head in, mouth covered with his shirt tail.

"Damn it, don't come in here, stupid ass old man," Joe scolds.

"Need to open them windows. Door too, maybe," Pop says.

"Don't need you to tell me that. Get the hell out before you burn something else up, you idiot."

Pop drops his head and retreats.

Joe opens the window above the sink and the door to the backyard. He sets an oscillating fan in the doorway to suck the smoke out.

Dee Dee Dog yaps somewhere behind the fence. Joe knows it's watching with an eye through the slats, alerting anyone within hearing range that the Salas' did something stupid.

Joe sets the fan farther out in the yard. Dee Dee Dog races back and forth behind the fence, its yapping morphing into a psychotic laugh.

Between the smoke alarm and the dog, Joe loses it. He grabs a galvanized garbage can near the back door and heaves it at the fence in the direction of the dog. It slams against the boards and the lid pops off slinging garbage down the fence line. Dee Dee Dog yelps as if it's been shot. Sounds as if it runs back to the house.

Things quiet some after that, except for the smoke alarm.

Joe takes the broom and marches through the kitchen into the dining room. With a brutal swing, one Pop would be proud of, Joe knocks the smoke alarm clean off the ceiling. The plastic cover hits the wall and shatters. The battery, still connected to wires, seeks refuge under the table like some mutant spider.

"Piece a *shit!*"

"What are we gonna do for a smoke alarm?!" Pop crows, his shirt tail in his hand, doughy stomach peeking beneath.

"I have an idea. How about you don't start any more damn fires!" Joe yells.

Pop collects the remains of the smoke alarm. "Not like it was done on purpose, JoJo."

Joe steps up and sweeps pieces of plastic from Pop's hand, "Leave it." Grabs the paper towels from the coffee table, notices he's written notes about Gyotaku on them—jeez! Glad he caught himself in time.

"My mess, I'll clean up. Can still do that," Pop mumbles.

"No, actually this one's mine. You scrub the damn skillet."

Pop nods towards the kitchen, "You gonna take care of that garbage? Helluva mess that one," he says, picking up little shards of plastic. Spots the battery under the table and points.

"Stink'll drive Dee Dee's dog nuts smellin' it all the time. Might start her bitchin'."

Joe fishes the battery from under the table with the broom. "She can kiss my ass."

"Wouldn't want that face near my ass, can assure you," Pop says limping back to the kitchen. Smiles when he says it.

Makes Joe smile, too.

keep the change

EUSTIS STREET GRILL, grey indoor-outdoor carpet, worn and stained. Eight tables with four chairs each, four booths covered in red vinyl. Abused plywood counter separates the dining area from the kitchen where the owner shifts from refrigerator to griddle as short order cook.

Every booth and table occupied, Joe inhales the aroma of bacon, home fries with onion and coffee. On the tables, lots of ketchup, and for the daring, Tabasco Sauce.

Betty's seated at the booth closest to the plate glass that exposes the street, the name of the diner painted at the top. She holds the newspaper, spread on the table, a cup of coffee steaming beside.

Joe slides in across from her, tries to read upside down. She glances up and smiles, closed lipped, self-conscious over the missing front tooth. Not so concerned with the keloids mapped across her face, regards them as war victories, but the missing tooth makes her feel damaged.

"Hey, JoJo, gettin' the usual?" she asks, reviewing the classifieds.

"Got a damn cold. Can't taste much. Too much smoke up my nose anyway." Joe's head settles low between his shoulders, hollow-chested, red nosed. Not unlike roosted vultures waiting for the prey to die.

"Smoke?" Betty folds the paper and sets it on the seat beside her. Leans in close to check Joe's red eyes. "You been smokin' dope? Piss me off if you're doin' it without me."

"Pop set the kitchen on fire."

"No, he didn't! Really?"

"Burned lunch. Not sure how that happened with him standin' there the whole time. Didn't lose anything. Just stunk things up." Joe digs through the little bag that hangs from his belt for cash, pulls out a ten and a sticky cough drop. Pops the cough drop in his mouth and slides the ten inside his glove.

Betty shakes her head, "Bless his heart. He sick, too?"

"Too mean."

Waitress steps up to the table, sets a coffee cup in front of Joe and prepares to write. "What can I get you today?"

Betty glances up, "Number four."

"Coffee's good, thanks," Joe adds. "Whatcha lookin' for in the paper?"

Betty starts on her coffee, "Nothin' really."

"I can tell when you lie. You don't do it very well, Betty girl."

"State's Attorney thought so. Cost me two years in prison."

"No, Ricky cost you two years in prison. He could've denied you had anything to do with it, but he didn't."

Waitress comes back with a coffee pot and fills Joe's cup. Tops off Betty's.

Joe dumps two creamers in his coffee, watches the white swirl into the black and turn caramel. He grits his teeth, "And about the paper?"

"Another apartment," Betty says.

"Why? You love that rat hole you're in."

"Can't believe you gave up yours to move in with Pop. What are you going to do about a job now?"

"Not worried about it. I got deposit money still."

"Always the detail shop. Good for quick cash," she tells him.

"Don't change the subject. Why a new place?"

"Don't want Ricky to find me. He'll hit me up for money I ain't got."

"Why would you consider even talking to that asshole? Tell him to get lost."

Waitress brings Betty's food, sets it in front of her.

Joe pulls the ten from his glove, slips it to her, and nods in Betty's direction. Waitress winks and moves on to another table.

"It's complicated." Betty eats two mouthfuls of eggs, "Can we not go into it now? Sure you don't want anything?"

Joe sits back in his seat, crosses his arms, and gives her a long silent gaze. "Yeah, sure," throws his hands up, "how about a fish?"

Bacon's crumbled over the last of the eggs and sprinkled with more salt. Betty stops chewing, "Fish? What do you want with a fish?"

"Experiment. An art thing maybe."

Her eyebrows scrunch together. "I'm not even gonna ask. I'll see what I can do."

POP LEANS ON his walkin' stick while moving from bush to bush in the back yard with his Fiskars by-pass clippers, trimming the ligustrum by hand, pulling a black garbage bag across the yard with him to collect the cuttings. The chore gives him a sense of peace and accomplishment he gets little of elsewhere.

He took yard work over after Mom died, his way of keeping her memory alive. He picked up where she left off a month after he'd put her in the ground. The lawn grew high and weedy, and the shrubs suffered from an insect invasion, all dying without her. He couldn't bear to watch them wither away, too.

Whenever he touches the leaves, or inhales the fragrance of the gardenias for just a moment, she's still alive as if they possess her energy and he can draw on it.

Out by the pond, three Sand Hill cranes forage at the water's edge. Blue jays call from the pines at the wood's line and woodpeckers rotate in and out of the dead pine to feed their chicks. Pop isn't sure how long he's been standing at the gate, the wind sighing through the pines, the smell of wet soil from the pond, whispers of past conversations he and Mom had about these very moments. He could relinquish his life right this minute and that would be okay with him.

Pop's revery explodes with a yapping, yapping, yapping from behind the fence. Dee Dee's let the dog out and it heads straight for the section of fence closest to Pop. The yapping turns to a distorted growl, with a strange pace to it, as if the beast were being shaken.

On the dog's side, front legs feverishly start digging, digging, digging to get under the fence.

Pop turns the hearing aid down and goes on with his trimming.

The gardenia's in full bloom, Mom's favorite. When the back door is open, the milky white clusters waft a fragrance that fills the kitchen. Pop checks its leaves for wooly bugs, unaware of the deepening hole under the fence, of the black nose crusted with sand.

He shuffles back to the kitchen for an ice tea, leaving the door ajar to catch the perfume of the gardenia and pulls a glass from the cabinet. He leans the walkin' stick against the counter and takes the tea pitcher out of the fridge, can't wait for the glass to touch his lips, the cool sweetness of the tea. But, he catches something out of the corner of his eye, a streak of black, a shift of light by the shed. He hesitates, puts the glass on the table and steps into the yard.

Wind blows through the River Birches and sweeps over the daylily bed, whispering echoes into his hearing aid. He turns back to the kitchen and the black streak moves across the yard. The dog lunges at Pop's bad leg, as if sensing the weakness in his hip, buckling the old man at the knee. Pop hits the ground. The dog goes for the right arm, shearing three inches of paper thin skin from the radial bone.

Pop gasps panicked whispers as the dog sinks his teeth in just above the elbow. Tissue tears away crimsoning Pop's shirt, the dog's teeth bathed in blood. Pop punches, drags himself to the house, pain in his chest, not enough air.

The dog stops, licks blood from its mouth, evaluates the situation. Pop's shaky scream for help sets the dog off again.

Dee Dee watches through the slats in the fence squeezing her balled up shirt tail in her thick hands, her breath quick, heart racing. She briefly considers calling the dog off. Almost calls its name. She shrugs, turns from the fence, smirks, glances around, sees no one. Returns to the house. Closes the door and locks it.

Pop lies at the back door out of breath, weak, pain in his ribcage eating him from the inside out. The dog attacks again, bites the back of his neck tearing the shirt at the collar, shreds the sleeve. Separates flesh from the upper shoulder. Teeth sink into his earlobe.

Pop crawls into the kitchen, grabs the table leg. The tea glass falls splintering across the floor.

THE SUN CASTS long shadows as Joe pedals up the driveway. House's dark, TV off. The back door stands wide open. Glass litters the floor like amber beads from the orange sunset spilling through the door. Under his feet a blood trail leads down the hall.

Joe pauses at Pop's open bedroom door. Honey sunlight filters through the mini blind slats, painting stripes on Pop curled in a fetal position on the bed.

Joe touches Pop's shoulder, feels him cringe. Thinks he hears a whimper and turns on the bedside lamp. "You all right?"

Bloody sheets. Bloody clothes. Joe goes weak in the knees. Bile rises in his throat. "Oh God," he whispers, "I'm calling 911."

"No, leave it!" Pop whispers.

"Gotta get you to a hospital."

"No damn hospital," Pop insists.

Joe doesn't know what to do first. The injuries are overwhelming. "What do you want me to do? You can't stay like this."

"Just clean it up some," Pop tells him.

Joe hurries to the bathroom and returns with a basin of warm water, Betadine, and the first aid kit. He cuts off the shirt and tends the worst wound first.

"This is gonna need stitches. I can't fix this." Joe's hand trembles around the Betadine bottle as he pours it in the gauze, his mouth dried to cotton. Gauze catches on the torn flesh and peels it back as Joe rubs the drying blood. He heaves once and swallows hard.

"What happened?" He places a large gauze pad on the wound and gently tapes it.

"The dog," Pop tells him.

"What dog?"

"Dee Dee's. Got in the back yard." Pop fades out.

Joe leans over to see if he's still breathing. It's heavy, but regular. Finishes tending the wounds and drapes the sheet over Pop's shoulders.

Joe goes to the back yard and finds the bloodstained wood and a hole under the fence. Through the slats, he sees Dee Dee giving the dog a bath in a large galvanized tub, blood on its fur, blood on the wash rag, blood trailing down her arm. Hears her coo baby talk as she rinses it off, wraps it in a towel, and scoops it up in her arms. The dog growls towards the fence, knows Joe's standing behind the fence, can smell the hate.

Dee Dee apologizes to the dog as if it's had a bad day and takes it back into the house.

For thirty minutes Joe stands by the fence chewing at a cuticle. Doesn't own a gun. Thinks of confronting her, threatening her with the police. She'd stand in the doorway and deny everything, swear the dog was with her the entire time. "Oh, hell no you don't. It wasn't my dog!" she'd say. The officer would say not much he could do since there were no witnesses. It would be Pop's word against hers. She'd be on guard after that. And careful. Better be.

8

felons, hamburger and pine sol

CIGARETTE SMOKE CURLS around the aluminum columns at the front door of Betty's rundown one-bedroom apartment. Ricky Vega sits on the concrete step in the dark, finishing his fifth smoke. His thumb and forefinger circle then flick the filter into the dark, the red tip dying in the dirt. A prison tattoo heals on his forearm, scabbed and red around the edges— a going away present from the bitches in cell block E.

He's only been out three days and already connected with his dealer and put the word out he's ready to take back what's his. Betty is next on the list.

With the cold dead eyes of a shark, he watches her walk up the sidewalk with her fishing gear, the water sloshing in the white bucket of crappies. He shifts smoothly out of the way, his sweaty prison-bulked biceps flexed and tense under his skin.

She doesn't notice him until she's almost on top of him. Starts, adrenaline burns her chest, dreads the moment he'll look in her eyes. Or worse, touch her.

"Wonderin' if you were coming home, Betty Boo. Aren't you glad to see me?"

Betty sets the bucket down and lays the poles against the wall. "What do you want?" She pulls open the screen door and sticks the key in the lock, reconsiders and pulls it back out.

"That any way to talk to your husband? I been dreamin' about this day, you and me. Pickin' up where we left off. Learned new tricks in the joint. Wanna see 'em?" He settles back grabbing his crotch, gives it a squeeze. Even in the dusk she sees his wide porcine grin, wonders how her life got sucked into his.

She focuses on the top of his greasy head, reeking with the stench of prison lovers. An image flashes through her brain, the different ways to assault the body, the variety of objects used when a penis is too worn out to perform. She senses, even in the dark, he's anxious to practice on her. "Divorced, remember?"

"Means shit to me," he says. "We'll always be together, me and you. We're connected."

"You signed the papers."

Ricky stands up, wipes his hand across his sweaty bare chest. "Wrong there, Betty Boo. I was under *duress.* Like that word? Means, I got pushed into it."

"I've gotten on with my life. It's not much, but it's mine," she says.

"Well, the way I see it, we got unfinished business and I mean to take what's mine. Unlock the door, girl. It's hot out here and I'm tired." He turns to the door and back again. "But not too tired for you."

JOE KEEPS HIS back door open most of the night, sitting at the kitchen table, watching the clock in the dark. Lightning bugs flicker in the shadow of the shed, frogs call from the pond.

He digs a hunk of ground chuck from the cello-pack and pats it onto a paper plate. Walks out to the yard and drops the plate a few feet in from the dig under the fence, then goes to the shed and unlocks it. He gropes straight to the tool bar with the light off and finds the shovel by feel. Closes the shed door, stands under the eaves and waits.

Dee Dee lets the dog out to pee fifteen minutes later. She closes the back door and turns off the light, leaving the dog to yap and shit at leisure while she goes back to bed ear plugged and beauty masked.

Dee Dee Dog makes the rounds, lifting its leg, pissing on the patio furniture, pissing on the concrete planter by the door, pissing on the hibiscus dying on the lawn. It sniffs the ground, turns in circles, arches its back and takes a dump next to a creepy stone-faced garden gnome. The dog catches the scent of meat; its nose, a Geiger counter, locks on. Critter squeezes through the hole dug under the fence, shakes itself off, puts its nose to the ground and follows it to the hamburger.

Joe, undetected, steps up behind as it gorges itself, lifts the shovel above his head and hits the dog between its perky ears with the metal spade, mouth still half full of raw burger. Kills it instantly.

Taking a deep breath, Joe pokes the carcass with his toe. "Shithead." Washes the shovel off with the water hose and puts it back in the shed, pulls a black garbage bag from the box on the work bench and locks up. He shoves the dog in the bag

48

and pauses. Doesn't know what to do with the body. He doesn't want the evidence around to be discovered when the fat bitch starts searching for her doggy poo, though the anguish on her face would go a long way toward making him feel better.

A whippoorwill calls out from the pond, begging, lonely.

Joe throws the bag over the fence and goes through the gate after it. Toting the bag, he works his way through the thick brush in the dark until he's at the foot of the dead pine, dumps the dog out, and kicks the carcass again to make sure it doesn't wake to return home and start up the misery all over again. Satisfied, Joe goes back to the house, throws the garbage bag and paper plate in the can and goes to bed.

POP DOESN'T MOVE all night. He's still asleep when Joe wakes up. Joe knows Pop's hurt worse than he's admitting, decides allowing the old man, with all his health problems, to play tough is not an option. Pictures Pop getting worse and being stuck tending after him day after day, no breaks, back and forth to the can, washing, cleaning, his life over until the old man dies. Hates the obligation chaining him down, hates the alternative of thinking the old man might die alone. Like it or not, he's the responsible one now.

The washer and dryer work non-stop for two hours cleaning bedclothes, pants, underwear, and bloody socks.

Before daybreak, Joe settles Pop into a warm tub to soak off dried blood. Tub is drained and refilled twice before the water runs clean. The arm wound's a traffic crash, continues to ooze. Pop agrees to a trip to the hospital, the pain worse than he'll admit. Joe packs a small overnight bag and makes a call to the VA hospital.

A bucket by the open back door is full of bloody Pine Sol water, broken glass at the bottom of the garbage can. Joe helps Pop to the kitchen table, takes the bucket to the back yard and slings the water over the fence.

"Need to call someone about the dog before it comes back." Pop yells from the doorway.

"No need. It's been taken care of."

"You talk to the Dee Dee woman?"

"I've handled it, Pop. It won't bother you or anyone else again."

Vultures drift in and start circling on the thermals above the pond. With each rotation they move in closer until one breaks away and sweeps over the top of the dead pine. On the third pass it lands.

Joe watches from the fence line, counts as four or five more vultures glide in. A swarm of black; cloistering, stripping, tearing, gorging soft organs, choice entrails. Joe turns back to the house.

Pop stands by the door clutching the frame, watching. They briefly make eye contact. Pop nods and goes back in.

"HE'LL NEED TO stay at least a few days, Mr. Salas. We want to be ahead of any infection. Place him on an IV drip. His wounds are serious enough to need close monitoring. At his age his immune system can't cope like yours or mine."

Joe and the doctor move against the wall as an empty gurney's wheeled past.

"His health has been declining over the past two years and this can get serious."

Joe listens, must have appeared as if he wasn't because of the way the doctor tilts his head and squints.

"Mr. Salas," the doc says tapping Joe's arm with a chart, "I think we got him in time. Why don't you go home? We'll call if anything develops. He's in good hands."

"I thought dogs had a special spit that healed wounds. What I'd always heard," Joe says. "Heard if you let a dog lick the wound it would heal right up."

"For the dog, but for people it's just a bacteria bath. It's an old wives' tale."

Joe nods. Feels stupid. Resents how the smell of piss and disinfectant takes him back to the day his Mom died. Different hospital. Same feeling.

A perky young nurse comes out, takes the chart from the doc, and fills in Pop's stats. "You can go in now, Mr. Salas. He's resting comfortably. He's on a pain medication and it might make him a little groggy. He should fall asleep soon."

In the eight-bed ward with pullable curtains between beds, Pop's lost in a sea of over baked linens. A plastic pitcher of water, small glass, plastic emesis pan sits on the wheelie table by the bed. An IV pole laden with bags of fluid, computerized monitor screen with codes, blips and buttons— Pop's personal support system.

Bandage wrappers and bloody gauze litter the floor for the orderly. Joe stands by the bed impatient to leave. He leans close to Pop's ear and whispers, "I'm goin' on, Pop. Just so you know, Sammy's still here."

Vile breath blows through Pop's open mouth, eyes quiver under the lids. His arm and shoulder have been stitched up and re-bandaged. No answer from Pop, his eyes crack open and rotate to the back of his head in a welcome drug-induced sleep.

The blips on the monitor seem regular enough. Joe inventories the room and the four other patients. Those still awake and alert gape back at him in blank resignation, waiting their turn at the *Movie.*

SHE'S NOT ANSWERING the phone. Answering machine isn't picking up, either. He hasn't heard from her in two days. It's not like Betty to be incommunicado. She doesn't vacation, has no family, no place to escape to other than her head. His gut has a bad feeling.

Joe pedals through the back streets to her apartment, finds her junker Chevy Nova parked in its spot on the street bleeding oil from the ports. Her fishing poles lean against the wall by the front door, her curled flip-flops on the welcome mat. This time of day she'd be on the dock unless her job called her in, which it never does. No real emergencies working the Laundromat.

The bucket sits by the poles, dead fish floating in stagnating water, four crappies that sucked all the air out of what little water they had. Now, Joe's really scared. He knocks on the door, tries to see any movement through the partially pulled curtains in the window. The second time he pounds on the door he puts his ear to it for any sound.

Door swings open in a whoosh. Betty stands holding the knob in a death grip.

"Where've you been?" he asks, shocked by the bruise that shadows her right eye and a swollen upper lip, wearing nothing but a bath towel.

"Go away, Joe," Betty hisses, trying to shut the door in his face.

Joe blocks it. "Hell no! What happened?"

"Nothing. I'll call you later." She avoids eye contact, tries to shut the door again.

Joe blocks it, sees she's pissed.

"Let him in!" Ricky yells behind her, all teeth, wet with sweat and sex. Wants Joe to know he's back, maybe pry details Betty's kept to herself. He pulls the door open and stands to the side in mock invitation.

Joe's hesitant, reads volumes into the few seconds the three of them stand in the doorway. It's bad for her, the hate, humiliation, and pain written all over her face. She doesn't need to explain. She'd warned him it was coming.

"Get us a beer, will you?" Ricky hawks.

As Betty turns for the bedroom, Ricky yanks the towel off. She stops and drops her head. Ricky wraps the towel around the back of his neck. "I'm back," he smiles. "Go on. Beer. And make it cold."

Betty bends down, bruises purpling her buttocks and thighs, plucks her torn clothes out of the hallway and disappears.

"So, they let you out." Joe sits on the arm of the sofa, scanning the room. One of the side tables is knocked over. Knickknacks and photographs of Betty with a little boy litter the floor. Pictures of the boy up to the age of four cluster on the coffee table like a shrine, burnt candles, a vase of dying flowers, small tattered teddy bears. Joe realizes Ricky's watching him.

"Turned the kid into a god, didn't she?" Ricky asks kicking the knickknacks across the floor. Snatches the picture off the floor and flops on the sofa. "Worships him more now than when he's alive. She needs to get the hell over it." Throws the photo back to the floor.

Joe doesn't know what to say. Knows he hates the guy, did the first time he met him. Shiftless. He'd called him that to his face once and Ricky beat the shit out of him for it.

"He was her son," Joe says.

"Our son," Ricky corrects.

"Then how do you think she'll get over somethin' like that?"

"I don't give a shit if she does or not. Not my problem now, is it?" he grins. "She's better off without him anyway.

Took up too much damn time. What you been up to these days?"

"Not much," Joe tells him, doesn't want this slime knowing anything about his business, certainly not his troubles.

"You been comin' 'round a lot? Takin' my place while I was gone?" Ricky savors the guilty looks sweeping Joe's face.

Betty brings in two beers and hands them out. She's dressed in more clothes than Joe's seen her in since winter.

"Askin' your boy here how long he's been sniffin' around. Bet you could answer that one, Betty Boo." Ricky waits, glances from her to Joe and back again. "Aw, you're no fun. So, JoJo, whatcha doing these days? Did I ask that one already?" He catches Betty's eye. "He didn't answer, Betty. Oh, that's right, you got canned, that right, JoJo?"

Betty's eyes sweep to Joe apologetic, she starts to move away.

"Get back here!" Ricky yells, flicks the anger back to a grin as if possessed by Mr. Hyde.

Joe jumps, acid filling his throat.

Betty steps back, stands by Ricky's chair like an obedient wife.

"See there, JoJo, just have to know how to train 'em. Now Betty Boo, what was it you were sayin' about old JoJo here? Oh, that's right. He got canned and had to move in with daddy. Must suck, livin' under daddy's thumb again." He grabs Betty's ass, watches Joe's face as he massages it.

Joe sets the beer on the table. "I'll catch up with you later, Betty." His foot bumps a photo of Betty and the boy at the boardwalk, fishing pole in the grinning toddler's hand. Joe bends down and picks it up. "His birthday's comin' up," he tells her. Purposely ignores Ricky.

She gives him a strained smile.

"Maybe we'll go celebrate, have a Jamie day." Joe sets the picture on the table.

"Don't think she'll be doin' no celebratin' with you," Ricky calls after him, "We got plans, but it was good seein' you again there, JoJo. Give my regards to your Pop."

Joe nods and closes the door behind him. He looks down at the bucket of dead fish. Purses his lips and nods again.

9

post-traumatic stress

LONG-TERM PATIENTS know who the lousy doctors are, watch their bedmates get probed as orders effect a quick release, whether out the door or to the morgue. If you're in the geriatric ward long enough you get to see plenty of them wheeled out dead. Get to know who has family, who doesn't.

One patient is the unofficial leader just for being there long enough to answer questions the staff won't. Like the truth about what meds they're giving you and what they're for, codes for mysterious medical terms, code blue always prefaced by a rush of personnel and mild panic as some poor bastard goes rigid in the bed, foaming at the mouth, a death grip on the bed sheet.

Some try to escape life without notice, but their monitors spy and tattle, snatching their suicide dreams.

Pop wakes in the middle of the night, disoriented. He raises his arm where a tube hooked to a needle is shoved into his hand. A good vein. Most collapsed years ago. If this one had failed, the nurse threatened him with the carotid artery.

56

He'd prayed to the vein, coaxing it to accept the needle, save him from the horror show he'd invented in his head about the needle missing its mark and him, alone in the dark, bleeding out.

Someone rustles in the bed at the far end of the ward. Pop can't see, can't raise his head. He feels around for the call button that dangles out of reach at the head of the bed. He hears a bed frame squeak, something knock into a side table, heavy breathing, water hitting the floor. Lots of it. A groan of relief. The bed frame squeaking again. Quiet. At some point shortly after, he drifts off again.

JOE SLIDES THE mail out of the box and locks himself in the house. It exhales cool piney breath from his earlier scrub down. He grabs a peach off the kitchen table and leans against the sink to eat it and read. By the time he gets to the sales advertisements, Dee Dee descends at the front door like a tornado, pounding and shrieking in her harpy voice.

"What did you do with him? Get out here and tell me what you did with him!"

Joe's head pops up like a wildebeest sensing danger at the watering hole. He knows she can't prove anything, but he's forced to deal with her, and hatches two or three plausible denials.

"I'm calling the police! You hear me in there?"

Joe jerks opens the door with the peach in his mouth just as her fist hammers the door again. Feels the breeze blow past his nose. He twists back, pulls the peach from his mouth. "What's your problem?"

"You know what my problem is! You got my dog and I want him back." She tries to enter the house. Joe blocks her, her face three inches from his nose, smells the ammonia dye from under the plastic shower cap. Henna red leaks from the cap and trickles down her temples.

"What are you talkin' about?"

Dee Dee snatches the mail from his hand, crushing it in her fist, "My damn dog. I know you did something to him, I can see it on your face."

"Why would I do anything to your dog? I don't even know you."

It stops her cold. She throws the mail to the floor. "Don't think for a minute I don't know you did something. I'll prove it and when I do, I'm pressing charges. I got friends in the police department. They'll listen to me."

Joe picks up the mail. "Pop's in the hospital. Might not make it. If he dies, the dog's the least of your problems."

"You threatening me?" she hisses.

"If I see your dog, I'll be sure to give you a call, *bitch.*" Joe shuts the door in her face, yanks it back open and hurls the peach. It rolls across the driveway.

Through the front window Joe watches her walk down the sidewalk, hands on her hips, scanning the street, shrieking for the dog.

Joe's tempted to run out, grab her by the back of the neck, and march her ass down through the brush to the foot of the dead pine, watch her eyes focus on the bones of her yappy bastard and realize she'd be next if she caused any more trouble.

There'd be a certain gratification in her worry, her heart breaking, the realization of her impending loneliness. But the fact she has friends in the police department doesn't sit well with him, wonders what he should do about it. Decides the dog business needs a plausible second escape route. God knows the dog had a reason to escape. That would end his involvement in the eyes of the law, knows she'd never mention that the dog mauled his father even if it gave him a motive to kill it.

Before going back to the hospital, Joe takes the shovel out of the shed and digs a hole outside Dee Dee's fence in the back yard by the thick woods. Makes it appear as if the dog had dug out and escaped. Any cop would buy it ten minutes with her.

IN HIS NIGHTMARE, Pop's screaming in his head that a man's down during a half day firefight in the third battle of Pork Chop Hill, Korea. Screams for Sarge. "Got to find a medic—my buddies lost an arm!" Pop yells in the ward. He shreds cloth for a tourniquet. Cowers from incoming artillery. Pain. Shrapnel's torn through his shoulder and earlobe.

A shadow looms over the bed, an aberration. When Pop opens his eyes, the shadow has eyes of its own, staring as if trying to penetrate his soul. The face begins to sharpen: distinct lines, intense eyes, facial stubble, bad acne scars. A white coat with unidentifiable stains, sleeves rolled up to the elbow, a name tag on which Pop can only make out the letters, LPN. Do jobs the RN's don't do anymore and given less respect. Moves from the bed in the dark and it sounds as if he's visiting each bed, checking vitals, checking IV bags for fluid content.

"Son of a bitch!"

Pop can't see what's happening, gropes for the hearing aid on the wheelie table. The boney fingers of his good hand pat around and knock the water pitcher to the floor.

Footsteps move quickly across the tile in a squeak squish, squeak squish and stop at Pop's bed. Pop hears the pitcher slammed down on the table, the shoes squeak by the bed. Heavy breathing.

"You old bastards do this on purpose, don't you? Don't want to screw with me today!" The LPN moves from the bed to the bathroom and turns on the light.

Pop sticks in his hearing aid, watches the silhouette against the bright fluorescents grab towels and return to his bedside. A towel drops to the floor, is squished around and picked up. Pop feels the shredded edges of the top sheet in his fingers, instinctively fears the LPN finding out about it. Slowly stuffs it under the thin blanket out of sight.

Across the room, Pop watches the illuminated faces of other patients, wide eyed and mute as if a shark trolls the aisles waiting for a hand to slip off the edge of the bed. The LPN returns to the bathroom and pulls a bucket from the cabinet, filling it with bleach and hot water. He takes the bucket and squeak squishes back to the end of the ward.

The light's too dim to make it that far and all Pop hears is water churning in the bucket and the wet towel smacking tile. Someone mumbles. A bedside table squeals on its castors and pushes against the metal bed rail. Painful moans. Silence.

"THEY CALL HIM Mister *Keys,"* an emaciated guy across the ward whispers to Pop, "you don't want to piss him off. He'll *do* things." He leans toward Pop, his fingers nothing more than onion skin over knotty bone, clutches the bed rail as if imparting national security intelligence. Gasps, pushes back in the bed and pretends to sleep.

Keys, the LPN, stalks through the ward. He's maybe thirty, stink eyeing the oldsters. Today's a bad day, Frank's fault for pissing the floor and not using the provided urinal bottle.

"Who are you!" Sammy yells from his bed to no one in particular.

"You know the routine, boys, don't make me do it for you," Keys instructs. "Hey Frank, they're operating today. Going to strip the steel from your dick."

Keys carries a crescent plastic emesis basin in which a can of shaving cream and a straight-edged razor stew in a wash of cold water. Sets the basin on the wheelie table by Frank's bed and drops the side rail.

"What's in the pan?" Frank asks.

Keys leans close to Frank's good ear, "Payback, baby." He pulls down the bed sheet and jerks up Frank's hospital gown. "Nothing to worry about. It's just a shave, Frank."

Frank leans over and sees the straight razor under the water. "What's that?"

"Just cream and a blade." Keys grabs Frank by the ankles and pulls him flat.

"Got to pee before we get started?"

Frank stares at the basin, glances at Keys. "Where's the safety razor, those disposables?"

"Don't worry, Frank. I've used it once or twice." Keys pulls Frank's knees up and shoves his legs apart. From the wince on Frank's face, it's been a long time since he's been spread-eagled like this.

Frank stares at the basin, his mind just short of panic. As Keys reaches for the razor, Frank slaps the basin off the table.

"You old *shit!*"

Keys collects the tools and returns to the bathroom to refill the basin. Frank, struggling, slowly rolls over and drops to the floor. He's weak and sits on the wet floor, spent.

The emaciated patient in the next bed pulls the oxygen mask from his face, stretches his neck and screams. "He's gettin' away! He's gettin' away, Mister Keys!" Throws off the sheet, "Mister Keys, he's making a break for it!" Takes a deep hit from his oxygen mask.

"Who are you!" Sammy yells.

Keys returns with the basin, "Good catch, Mick," and quickly sets it down, grabs Frank under the arms and heaves him back in bed. Frank's too exhausted to fight.

"That was a stupid thing to do, Frank. You know what that means." He pulls out the restraints from the bed frame and ties down Frank's wrists and ankles. Hitches the gown up and lifts the razor from the basin.

"Don't move, Frank. It's a little rusty and it's been a while since I've used this." The razor doesn't lock and flops around in his hand. "We'll have that hair off in no time."

Frank writhes in fear, gripping the mattress, his face drained of blood.

"A little foam to grease up this bad boy," Keys mutters. Wipes foam around Frank's penis and begins to carve the hair away.

"Oops, sorry about that, Frank."

Frank goes rigid on the bed. A solitary tear trails into his ear.

Keys dips the razor in the basin, turning the water pink. Hair floats to the top. "Almost done." Blood feathers like capillaries into what foam is smeared on Frank's thigh.

Keys drops the razor into the basin and carries it to the bathroom, makes sure everyone on the ward sees it. "My day's getting better, boys." He comes back with a bandage, small brown bottle of Merthiolate—ten percent alcohol and acetone. Unscrews the cap and pours the entire contents on the razor cut. Frank screams.

"Stop, you big pussy." Keys packs the wound with gauze, wipes away the excess shaving cream, and leaves the ward for breakfast trays. Leaves Frank naked and cold with the hospital gown still up around his neck.

Pop sits up on his elbow for a better view, can see the old guy quivering, probably crying. He lies back down and pulls the sheet over his shoulder, prays he's released soon.

"What'd you do that for?" Pop asks, peering through the bed rail. Glares at bigmouth Mick sucking air from the mask, his chest heaving for every precious breath.

Mick stares back, desperate. Pulls the mask from his face, leans over to be sure Keys is out of the room. "You'd do it too. Like any one of us," takes a drag from the mask again. "Been here a month," points to his chest, "emphysema. Not walkin' outa here and I know it. Keys treats us better if we cooperate."

Mick points to Cecil, the moribund diabetic in the bed next to Pop. "He's next," gasps, "Frank took Cecil's place because Frank pissed the floor." Mick respires, hand trembling around the mask so bad Pop thinks the poor bastard's gonna pass out.

The surgical team, dressed in green scrubs, shoe covers, and surgical hats, enters the ward and unhooks Frank's lines. He's blessed with a sleepy shot and wheeled out.

"What's Frank got?" Pop asks Mick.

"Got the cancer. Gonna cut it out. Heard the nurse tell Keys it spread all over, but they're gonna cut him anyway." Winks as if Pop's supposed to know what it means.

Mick holds the mask to his face, raises a hand. Flops back on the pillow, his entire body rocking from lung spasms. The blips on his monitor come fast and erratic.

The nurse rushes in, adjusts Mick's air supply and gives him an injection that knocks him out.

Pop looks over at Cecil in the next bed. He's a very old guy losing toes to gangrene, a lousy heart, and dementia from being in bed so long that they've more or less given up on his bed sores. Tubes shoved in his bladder run pink into a container clipped to the bed. His fingernails, yellow and curled, leave gouges on his neck because sometimes at night he feels like he's being suffocated.

Other than injections into his IV port, nothing much gets done with the old guy. He sleeps the better part of eighteen, twenty hours a day, doesn't speak, doesn't touch the food tray, and is berated like a toddler for not eating.

Almost a week now, nutrition is forced into his system through a clumsy feeding tube shoved into his nose. They'd prefer him to feed on solids; Keys, hating the bed stripping and ass wiping before the wheeling to dialysis, doesn't care that the old guy's in a deep depression.

Cold fear washes through Pop. Counts the minutes until Joe shows up to take him home, tells himself the intense pain in his arm is part of the healing process.

10

moldy addictions

WASN'T SURE WHY he didn't think of it earlier. The likeness on the tablet is a little creepy (perfect bow lips, chubby cheeks, curly blonde hair), but the eyes follow him around the room.

Joe shades in the strap on the overalls, signs his name, and adds, *Love Always, Joe*. He'll take it to the park by the lake where Betty watches kids playing on the jungle gym and give it to her.

He's spent every birthday for the past two years at that park on a promise to Betty while she languished in state prison for an armed robbery conviction. Authorities didn't care she was just the driver with no guilty knowledge of Ricky's intentions. Sentenced and convicted her just the same. Her instructions to Joe had been explicit. Don't visit until her release. Just toast Jamie at the park on his birthday.

Joe slides the drawing into the portfolio on his bike and heads for the park.

GET HIM DRUNK enough and time is on her side. An old trick Betty had learned from her abusive alcoholic father. Ricky's spread, passed out, on the bedroom floor, gut filled with a six-pack of beer and three quarters of a bottle of Old Turkey.

Betty closes the bedroom door and dresses. She goes to the hall closet, takes a brown paper bag from the shelf and tucks it under her arm. As she leaves the house, she tries not to think about the vicious cycle her life has become, but she can't help noticing an irony. Like an addiction, she's attracted to what hurts her most, as if it's all she deserves.

She finds Joe sitting on the lakefront bench watching sailboats trim through the water, seven, maybe ten of them. She sits next to him, pours gin into a second paper cup she's tucked into the first and hands it over.

Betty relies on Joe's support, even more on this day than on the usual anniversary of Jamie's death.

"Forgot to tell you the other day, I put Pop in the hospital," Joe says squinting at the lake, doesn't want her feeling pressured by what happened at her apartment. He hears the crinkle of the paper bag, knows what's inside.

"What's wrong?"

"Dog got him," drinks from the paper cup. "Tore him up good."

"Where'd the dog come from?"

"Doesn't matter," Joe tells her, throat burning from gin. "Not a problem anymore."

"He allowed visitors?"

"He wouldn't want people he knows seein' him that way."

Joe sets the cup on the edge of the bench, takes the bag from her hand and opens it. It's his turn this year. Out comes a matted, mildew-stained, stuffed bunny with a missing eye. The left ear hangs by a thread threatening to fall off.

"Need to sew this," Joe says, squeezing the ear to the head as if it'll miraculously stick. He knows she won't sew it. She fears changing it in any way will curse it, curse the child, curse her. Joe holds the bunny up to his face. "Could use a bath."

Betty reaches over and rubs the bunny's face. "He'd drool on it. Sucked the ear to put himself to sleep. That's why it's falling off like that. I hide it now. Ricky'll throw it out. Or worse, make me throw it out. Stand over me while I do it.

"What did you see in that guy?" Joe lays the bunny on his lap.

For what seems a long time, Betty gazes out at the water. Thunderheads build across the lake in a great plume of purple clouds. "What other stupid girls see. He was good looking, romantic, said all the right words. Promised me the sky if I wanted it."

"Why did you stay with him? Even after you knew what he was?"

"It's complicated. And it wasn't always about me."

"You stayed for Jamie?"

Joe sees she's distressed, hands the bunny back. "Never mind. None of my business. Just hate to see you so miserable." He reaches over and pulls the drawing out of the portfolio. "Drew this today. Thought you might like it. Done in charcoal, but I sprayed it so it won't smear." He holds it up, distracted by a strange nervousness in his gut. Bites his thumb nail.

She doesn't say anything, and with a shaky hand, takes the drawing from him. Laying the bunny on her lap, she holds the drawing with both hands, eyes glistening. "This is really good, JoJo. I'm proud to have it."

"He'd be what, six today?" Joe asks more to himself out loud, watching two little boys on bicycles trade candy, teasing, loud. "About their age."

Betty imagines Jamie among them, can see his dimples, the cowlick that stuck straight up above his forehead. At six it might not have been so conspicuous anymore, but she'll never get the chance to find out. She doubles over, the bunny crushed to her body, and sobs.

Joe puts one arm around her, furtively brushes a tear running down his cheek.

"SALAS...ANTHONY. Dog bite. Bet it hurts." Keys reviews the chart, gets to work. He strips the paper wrapper off the gauze bandage, sets it aside, takes the plastic cover off the hypodermic and sets it next to the bandage. Cuts along the bloody bandage stuck to the wound on Pop's arm. With a faint smile, Keys rips it off. From Pop's expression, it hurts. A lot.

"Oh, stop now. It wasn't that bad. Better to rip it off fast, what I always say."

"Saw you cut him on purpose," Pop says, his hand shaking.

"You don't know what you saw old man. That's the thing, you know? Get old, eyes are shot, it's dark, you're medicated, maybe dreaming," Keys mutters while cleaning the arm, isn't particularly gentle about it. Has such a tight grip on Pop's wrist, it goes numb with a weird throb in the fingers.

Pop wants to pull away, but Keys is young. And strong.

Pop hisses, "Bastard like you should be court-martialed and shot!"

"Well then, it's a good thing I'm a civilian, isn't it?"

"Got another thing comin if you think you can bully me."

Keys rewraps the wound, "Really? You're a real badass I bet. A hundred and twenty-pound ass kicker, you are."

"Tellin' the doctor when I see him."

Keys pours alcohol on the gauze and scrubs Pop's ear. Gives it a nice *pinch*.

Pop tries to fight, but Keys fingers wrap around his skull holding him down like great talons.

"Another wound on the shoulder," Keys asks, "right?"

"Leave it be," Pop begs.

"Oh, no, we can't do that. I wouldn't be doing my job. You see, I take a lot of time with my patients. See they get the special treatment they need."

"Bastard. Not gettin' away with it."

"You need pain medication," Keys says. He takes the hypodermic and holds it up. Pushes out the air and stabs the needle into the arm wound. Right through the bandage.

Pop's chest heaves. He starts to scream.

Keys covers Pop's mouth with a latexed hand. "Let's not upset the others. Almost dinner time. Turkey, I think."

Gathering his tray, Keys pulls the curtain around Pop's bed and stalks out of the ward.

SOMETIME AROUND TEN, Pop wakes, fear creeping across his chest. He can tell the general time of night by inactivity in the ward. He's missed dinner, suspects he got more in his injection than painkiller.

It's dark, just two small lights on over Mick's and Cecil's beds. Pop's curtain has been pulled back since he passed out and the ward's clear of dinner trays and visitors—that's if there were any. He seems to be the only one who gets visitors, wonders how the story goes with the rest of them.

A Kmart bag sits on his nightstand holding fresh underwear and a pair of socks. Joe must have dropped by while he was out of it. He's more than a little disappointed he's missed Joe's visit and won't see him until tomorrow.

Frank hasn't come back from surgery. Pop thinks he must be recouping in intensive care and looks over at Cecil, torpid, mouth open, eyes closed. Pop thinks he might be dead, but the monitor shows regular blips. Can barely see his chest rising.

Cecil hasn't moved or said a word since he was admitted. Sammy's been hooked to more cables and IV bags since this morning and doesn't wake up anymore.

Mick's staring at him, the oxygen mask strapped to his face just in case his lungs spasm again. Fear floats behind his eyes.

"Mick, what's wrong?" Pop asks.

Mick quickly shakes his head.

"Where's Frank?"

Mick pulls down the mask, leans over, and looks down the ward. "Keys says he died on the table."

Pop looks over at the empty bed. Sheets are clean and tight on the mattress. Fresh fluffed pillow. The monitors all shut off and pushed against the wall, the side table empty. The wheelie table sits neatly in the corner. All Frank's stuff's gone.

Mick makes eye contact. Pop wishes he hadn't. It's brutal in its implication, swings wide the swath of doom and fear Pop thinks has broken free from his nightmare and infected the ward. Mick lies back and fits the mask on his face.

Pop, too, lies back and pulls the sheet up to his chin. He starts thinking about his missed meal, wonders if Joe might sneak him something in. One of those monster burgers from the diner. He reaches for the phone. It's been removed.

The door to the ward opens and then closes again. Keys, smirking, walks past Pop's bed carrying a dessert— shortcake surmounted by a good six inches of whipped cream and crowned with fresh strawberries in a pressed glass sundae dish.

Keys holds the dish in front of Cecil's face and pushes the button that cranks him up to a sitting position. Then plunks the dish down and watches.

The diabetic opens his eyes and thinks he must be dreaming. Takes notice of the world for the first time in days, reaches for the graceful long-handled spoon. Keys snatches the treat away. "You got to be crazy thinking you can eat something like this. Dietitian made a mistake." He takes the dessert over to Mick. "Accidentally gave this to Cecil. He started on it, but it's almost all here." Wipes off the spoon under his armpit and offers it to Mick.

Mick shakes his head no, eyes above the mask the size of saucers.

"Sure?" Keys turns to Cecil, scoops up a huge spoonful and starts eating it. Whipped cream oozes from between his lips. He lowers Cecil's bed back down, strawberry juice rolling down his chin while the motor pulls the bed flat again.

Cecil gropes half blindly after the retreating form, moans as Keys leaves the ward savoring the shortcake.

"That's one evil son-of-a-bitch, if you ask me," Mick says, holding the mask from his face. "Hey Cecil, how you doin'? Mean thing that Keys did to you."

Cecil's head slowly turns to Pop. He whispers something Pop can't hear, his hand shaking like he's got something he wants to say. Pop crawls out of bed, watching the door. He nears Cecil's bed and leans close to the old guy's face, puts his ear to his mouth and listens.

Mick scoots down towards the end of his bed trying to hear, oxygen mask stretched to its limit to watch facial expressions. "What he say?"

Pop's head comes up slowly, stares at Cecil.

"What he say?" Mick gasps again, grabs his mask and takes a hit.

"He said… 'we're all dead.'"

11

animal police

AN ANIMAL CONTROL Officer is in Dee Dee's driveway when Joe rolls in. A middle-aged black woman in brown shorts and uniform shirt leaning against the driver's door, arms crossed with an expression of helplessness. She's too heavy to be out working in Florida's humid heat, sweat bleeding through the uniform's armpits and chest. She constantly blots her face with a hand towel to capture itchy sweat glistening at the temples.

Dee Dee has her pinned down against the city truck, pointing to Joe's house. When Joe gets out of the car he hears his name, pretends none of this has anything to do with him, unlocks the door and slides inside.

Before he gets to the kitchen, the bell rings. The officer stands with one hand on the door frame, the other clutching the towel, tilts her head into the cool draft from the open door. Joe can tell she wants in, if for nothing more than an opportunity to cool off and get away from Dee Dee. He feels for her.

"Can I help you?" he asks, knows why she's at his front door, can see in her eyes she just wants to clear the call.

"I been talking to your neighbor and she's missing her dog. You familiar with it?"

"Umm, seen her with it now and then. She told me about it missing yesterday. Don't know any more than what I told her before. Like to come into the cool?"

"That would be nice. And you are?" she holds out her hand.

"Joseph Salas. Call me Joe. Friends do." Gives her hand a gentle squeeze.

"Officer Lakisha Hicks, Eustis Animal Control. We got this call in a roundabout way. She called the P.D. and insisted on seeing an officer, so dispatcher referred her to me. Owes me big for this one."

"What's this got to do with me?" Joe sits on the arm of the sofa and folds his arms across his chest.

"She seems to think you've done something to her dog."

"Done what?"

"Doesn't know. Taken it off somewhere and dumped it off. Or worse." She wipes drying sweat from her forehead.

"Why would I bother her dog? See, I've only lived here a few weeks. Really don't know the woman. See her at the mailbox. See her with it when she waters the lawn. Dog's never done anything to me."

"You live here alone, Joe?" she asks, looking over him into the dining room.

"With my father. He's in the hospital. He's been in and out lately with health problems."

"Sorry to hear that. He ever have problems with the dog?"

Joe reads her face for any indication she might already know the answer to the question, a question that feels vaguely like the kind of trap cops use to further their investigations. Joe raises an eyebrow.

"I know. Had to ask," she says waving her hand, "We get complainants like her all the time if you can believe that. I'd much rather deal with the animals if you know what I mean."

Joe rubs the back of his neck, "Has anyone considered that maybe it ran off?"

"As a matter of fact, I did suggest that to her and she insists it wouldn't do that."

"Did you check? I mean, could it have knocked the guard out, stole his uniform and slipped by undetected?"

Her eyes flash from confused to surprised, then she laughs. "You're a funny man. If it was me, I would a used whatever means it took to get away. But it's my job to check it out, and check it out is what I'll do. Mind if I snoop around your back yard, see the fence between your properties?"

"Sure," Joe tells her. He stands up and walks her through the house, sees her noting things around the room as she goes. "We can go through the gate at the back. There's a firebreak dug out by the forestry people that's cut along the back of everyone's property here." Joe opens the back door.

"This is really nice back here," she says. Puts her hands on her hips and surveys the yard and the woods beyond the gate. "I bet you just love it here."

Joe leads her to the gate and opens it. "Folks did. Mom was into gardening."

"I can see that. Real nice. How long they live here?" Officer Hicks bends down and starts checking the fencing.

"A good fifty years." Joe drops back, gives her space to do her job.

"Know the rest of your neighbors?"

"Other than Dee Dee, the rest of 'em go up north for the summer," he says.

When they get to Dee Dee's fence, Officer Hicks stops. "Well I'll be. It's a nice hole, too." She kneels and brushes her fingers through the loose sand, checks up and down the fence line. "Run off is just what that little bugger did." She stands up with great effort, wipes her face with the towel. Joe stands propped against the fence, shrugs his shoulders.

"Good. I can go back to the office. She'll be heartbroken, but at least I can tell her we'll be on the watch for it. It'll show up—that is if someone doesn't steal it," she says walking through the gate. She eyes the fence, eyes the shed. "What do you keep in there?"

"Usual crap. Tools mostly, storage for stuff there's not room in the house for."

"Always keep it locked?" she asks holding the padlock in her palm.

"Unless I'm working in it or Pop's gardening. Think I got the dog in the shed?"

"She does. Mind?"

Joe smiles, "Not at all." He separates the shed key from his key ring and opens the door. Switches on the light. Most of the smell's faded, replaced with stagnant air and plastic containers neatly stacked along the wall.

She inspects every wall, every tool, every container, even the sink. "Nice little shop here. My dad's got a shop like this, but he fixes cars. You know, junkers no one else wants? He takes it in, loves it, sells it. Sometimes," she laughs, "more lovin' than sellin'."

"Pop built this twenty, thirty years ago for my Mom. He doesn't spend much time in here anymore since she died," Joe says.

"No? That's too bad. Sorry to hear about your Mom. Well, I can tell your neighbor I've solved the mystery and be on my way. Thank you for being so understanding. It's made my job much easier and I really appreciate it."

Joe locks up the shed, sees Officer Hicks walking down the fence line, poking the bottom of the wood with her steel toed boot. The hole where the Dee Dee dog had dug under it is refilled on both sides. A little job executed in the wee hours of the morning while Dee Dee slept off her Xanax.

On his side, Joe has transplanted a gardenia bush. The heavy aroma tempts Officer Hicks to bend down and smell the blooms. Joe snaps one off and hands it to her. "Put this in water and set it on your desk. Smell will fill the whole room."

"Why, thank you, Mr. Salas. How sweet." She starts for the back door, notes the dead pine at the pond. "What's down there?"

"Swamp, dying trees, snakes."

A lone vulture perches at the top of the pine, wings spread, catching the breeze. "I get more complaints about them birds," she says. "And there's not a thing in the world I can do."

"They don't bother anyone," Joe says opening the back door.

"Do if you keep a boat on the river. For some reason they like vinyl. Like seat cushions, pipe insulation, even roofing material. You believe that? Been told it emits a smell like rotten flesh to them. I don't know. I keep clear," she says walking through the house.

At the door Joe asks, "This put an end to it?"

"As far as the city's concerned. I feel for the sister, but I can't stand around and hold her hand. She'll need to find another dog," rolls her eyes, "or a man. Have a nice day."

Officer Hicks chuckles as she walks back to Dee Dee's front door and knocks. Joe watches from the front window, sees Dee Dee isn't happy with the results. She bolts from the door and runs on her stubby legs through her side gate to the back yard.

76

Officer Hicks sits in her truck, air on full blast and fills out her report.

Joe can't help it. He goes to the back yard, peers between the slats in the fence as Dee Dee paces back and forth in front of the newly discovered hole. She spins on her swollen little feet and turns in Joe's direction as if she knows he's standing there gloating. She stomps back to the house and slams the door hard enough to rattle the plate glass.

12

dreams in the freezer

HE DREAMS A shadow lurks in the ward drifting from bed to bed. It stands at Sammy's bed, fondles the IV tubes, and Pop thinks he sees the shadow stick something in its pocket. A nightmare, he tells himself, and fades out again.

Restless and inflamed, Pop's sleep leaves him weak and he doesn't know why. Suspects it was the medication dumped into his IV port sometime around midnight. When fully awake, he notices Sammy's empty bed, clean sheets pulled tight to the mattress, pillow fluffed. Some of the equipment's missing. All Sammy's personal stuff, too.

Pop sits up clutching the bed rail, looks over at Cecil's bed. He's gone, too.

Mick shuffles out of the bathroom dragging his oxygen bottle, the back of his gown wide open, toilet paper wedged in the crack of his ass.

Looking around for Keys, Pop asks, "Where's Sammy and Cecil?"

Mick shuffles to Pop's bed, "Sammy kicked it. Sometime around two. Heard him gaspin' for air. Keys came in, just shut everything off, and wheeled him out," presses the mask to his face for air, inhales five or six times and pulls it off. "Took Cecil out this morning."

"He dead too?"

"Don't know. If he is, that just leaves us." Mick starts trembling from standing so long. "Gotta get to the bed. Not feelin' so well."

Pop thinks about what Cecil had said. Squeezes his eyes shut.

IT'S A SMALL freezer chest. Not big enough to hold a side of beef, but big enough for a few months' worth of prime cuts and fresh-picked summer produce, blanched and bagged for the winter, if that was what one wanted to use it for.

A rusted exterior, corroded chrome handle, dents in the side and back left corner crumpled from being dropped off the back of a truck. The interior smells of mildew and rot. The three boxes of baking soda at the bottom don't help much, either. But Joe's been assured the compressor's good as new. Found it in the Thrifty Dollar, a throwaway newspaper advertising products and services for folks searching for second hand items and odd jobs.

Joe barely gets it wedged in the trunk of Pop's Buick. Buys it with part of his apartment deposit money. He thinks about needing to find a job as he straps the rope down. Then he thinks about his artwork, or lack thereof, and that gets him thinking about why he bought the freezer in the first place.

Pop's release is imminent and Joe needs to get it in the shed and hooked to power before he picks him up.

He's been working in the shed the entire afternoon, rearranging, setting up more lighting. Even installed a stronger lock on the door. When he goes to pick up the freezer, the guy stares at him kind of sideways and says, "What's wrong with your face there?"

Joe puts his hand to his cheek wondering what might be wrong. It dawns on him all the paint didn't scrub off. "Paint," he says.

"Fall on ya or somethin'?" the guy asks.

"Art. I'm an artist. It's an experiment. Sort of."

"Doesn't look like it worked out for ya."

No comment from his end. Joe hands the guy two tens and a five and drives off with the freezer tied in the trunk, the trunk lid bouncing.

As soon as he pulls up in the driveway, Dee Dee makes a point of going to the mailbox, takes her time opening it, watching Joe from the corner of her eye. Five minutes to retrieve two fliers and the phone bill. Longer to peruse them. His car has blocked her view from the front window and she's dying to see what he's brought home. Thinks it has something to do with her dog. Her mouth drops open when she spots the freezer.

Joe glances up at that precise moment then down at the freezer. Reads her mind. "Damn dog's not in here," he says.

Her mouth snaps shut and she scowls back just knowing the dog's either in there, or going to be. Joe barks and growls at her. She jumps and hurries back in the house.

He straps the freezer to the dolly and wheels it to the back yard, hears Dee Dee's glass door slide open as he unlocks the shed.

She appears on the edge of the patio as if she's afraid she'll be eaten if she sets foot on the grass, stretching her neck for a view of what he's doing. Listens intently for the dog. For a whimper. For a desperate muffled bark. She can't gather the nerve to peer through the slats. She hasn't gotten that desperate yet. Doesn't want to give the son of a bitch the satisfaction of knowing she's really in pain and knowing he's the reason. Feels it's up to her to investigate what no one else seems to want to.

A hole under the fence. Doesn't buy for a minute that the dog dug free and never came back. Even if the dog did dig out, she concludes, it would certainly come home for dinner. Not giving any more money to the damn Police Benevolent Association, either.

Joe closes himself in and gets to work. The freezer starts to cool minutes after getting power. Within an hour the smell's not so bad.

He's been dragging stuff down from the house. Pins and needles from his mom's old sewing kit, Q-tips and cotton balls, paper towels, a shallow soda flat (24 cans) and art materials from his old apartment, his easel, box of acrylic paints, sketch books, gesso, a dozen different pens and pencils.

Using his returned deposit money has given him enough cash for new materials: rice paper, block printing ink, fabric acrylics. Remembers he's left a roll of plastic sheeting in the back seat of the car.

Pulling the roll of sheeting from the back seat, it slips from his hands and unrolls into the street. He's forced to re-roll the entire thing, notices Dee Dee standing at her front window, hand covering her mouth in horror. He grabs a corner of the plastic and shakes it at her.

COMPLAINING TO THE nurse about Keys turns out to be a bad idea. Pop isn't privy to the fact she's a "good" friend of Keys, and that she and all the nurses damn near worship the ground he walks on. He takes good care of the girls, covers for them when they screw up, changes flat tires in the parking lot, buys espressos during breaks, services the lonely ones. A real politician.

Nurse goes straight to Keys and tells him everything. Pop should've asked Mick first, but Mick's undergoing some procedure to help his lungs. So, Pop was told. Had Mick known, he would have told Pop to keep his trap shut until he was released. Too late now.

The moment Keys appears at his bedside Pop knows the cat's out of the bag. Knows because Keys sneers and doesn't speak. Just like with the others. Keys pulls a hypodermic from his pocket and pops off the cap, doesn't even bother to push the air out, at least Pop doesn't see him push it out, and stabs him in the thigh right through the sheet. No time to scream. Next thing Pop knows he's feeling dizzy and his throat tightens up, it's hard to breathe. And the lights go out. Deep in the bowels of his dream the code blue alarm goes off.

JOE HAS NOTE-written paper towels spread across the kitchen counter when the call comes. Pop's had an *"episode."* That's what they call it so it won't sound as bad as saying he's coded once or twice, but by the grace of God he's still alive.

Staff at the nurse's station is gathered laughing and horsing around as if it's been a boring day and they need something to break up the monotony. Joe stands trying to be polite, but after five minutes of being ignored, he's sick of it and grabs a nurse's aide by the forearm, squeezing until the guy realizes it hurts.

"What's Mr. Salas' condition?"

Aid nods towards the room. "He's resting," he says, pulling his arm away.

"What happened?"

"I, I don't know. I wasn't there. Maybe you can ask his doctor," aid says smiling at the others like it's a private joke and he isn't going to share with Joe.

Where is he?"

"On the floor somewhere." Aid rubs his arm, tilts his head at the nurses and disappears down the hall.

Joe finds Pop on a respirator, hooked to more IV's, greyer, thinner than the last time he visited. He pulls a chair to the bed, sits, and takes Pop's hand.

Seeing the old man vulnerable and weak hurts him, remembers him as a younger man, always ready to kick someone's ass. Not like now, as if life has kicked his.

Joe's in an odd place, a reversal of roles, one he'd not bought into. He thinks how he by now should be married with kids, maybe with a studio, a teaching one, a retirement plan and a few stocks to play with. Instead he's unemployed, broke, and alone with this old man who never thought his son was good enough. Maybe the old man was right. Maybe sensed it from the beginning, how he'd waste his life pursuing an elusive dream, never having a stable career or family. But he's all the old man has left.

Joe thinks of his Mom and remembers her in a place like this, on the same machines, thinking she'd be coming home, but she never did. And he never said what she needed to hear.

"Hey Pop." Joe scans the room, sees the rest of the ward's empty. Thinks maybe now he has the nerve to say things to his unconscious father, things that might embarrass him if said to his face, but Keys suddenly appears over his shoulder.

"How's he doing?" Keys checks Pop's pulse.

"You tell me." Joe watches Pop's eyes flutter.

"Looks like our boy is trying to come out of it. We'll pull that tube out in a few hours." Keys adjusts the IV drip rate and squeezes Joe's shoulder. "Doc will be in soon."

"What happened? Why's he on a respirator? He came in here for a damn dog bite," Joe says. He's a head taller than Keys, but Keys has more weight on his bones. Lifting geriatric patients for two years has beefed up his upper body and forged his hands into steel vice grips Joe can feel as Keys releases his shoulder.

"Had a minor reaction to some medication."

"Exactly what medication?"

"Probably the penicillin."

"He's allergic to penicillin. It's in his chart. Has a bracelet. No one noticed?"

"I'm not at liberty to discuss it. Need to take it up with the doctor."

"Like hell. Who's the stupid-ass who can't read?" Joe moves into Keys' face, sees something alien lurking behind the eyes.

"I've got another patient," Keys says quietly. Stares at Joe in his alpha dog way until Joe feels uncomfortable enough to back off and let Keys go back to patients.

Joe stands next to Pop's bed, angry. He feels the same way about Keys that he does about Ricky, that they're cut from the same cloth.

It's after visiting hours before Joe sees the doctor. He's told the standard, *"We're investigating it"* crap.

"How'd he get the penicillin?" Joe asks.

"Not sure. The wrong hypo could've been picked up by accident."

"Who gave him the injection? You?"

"No. We're checking into it. Point is he's fine and should be released tomorrow." Doc slides from the question like he's swathed in Crisco.

"Point is it shouldn't have happened in the first place. Maybe I should find a way to correct that mistake."

"That's your right, Mr. Salas, but experience has shown that unless you've suffered some permanent damage, a monetary settlement isn't likely. And it's expensive."

Joe reads between the lines, hears the Doc telling him he's too poor to afford a long drawn out legal battle with the Federal Government that fights and squashes nuisances like him on a daily basis. Joe fumes just under the surface. "Don't believe I said anything about a lawsuit."

There's a long silence. Dead air. Doc dispenses with the hand shake and leaves Joe standing with no straight answers and no accountability.

Joe watches the jerk of the respirator and rise and fall of Pop's chest. He's scared for the old man and sits back in the chair holding his hand, feels the loose skin over a hand once strong and protective. After an hour, he kisses Pop on the forehead and goes home.

JOE CAN'T SLEEP. He sits at the kitchen table, back door open, watching fireflies and drinking beer. He wants to call Betty, even picks up the phone, but knowing her problems, decides against it. Truth is he doesn't want Ricky between them. Instead, he goes to the shed, closes himself in, turns on the light, goes to the freezer and retrieves a small fish wrapped in aluminum foil. He sets it on the work bench; and as it thaws out, reads over his notes on the paper towels inventorying the needed art material.

The fish is supposed to have good definition. First words on the paper towel. Joe's not sure if this one's definition qualifies. It's his first attempt at Gyotaku. He's not even sure what kind of fish this is, just something bought from the seafood counter at Albertsons. The only whole fish they had. Betty was supposed to supply a fresh one, instructions said to use a fresh one, still alive if possible, but she has her own issues and he isn't going to bug her now about a damn fish.

He'd smeared paint on the side of his face a few days back and tried to transfer it to paper, but it lost something in the translation. Red dye still shadows his skin as if sunburned.

Twenty minutes into it, the fish has become somewhat malleable, but leaks. He must continually paper towel off icky fish exudates that keep the paint from sticking. Already, the whole procedure is losing its thrill.

Frustration overwhelms him, anger at the hospital, his dead-end art career, the return of life long enemy Ricky, and a next-door neighbor determined to make his life miserable. Joe stabs a flathead screwdriver into the fish, ruining it. There's a weird kind of release in it, small but satisfying. He stabs it again and again until it's nearly cut in half. Joe sinks to the floor exhausted, fish skin and scales stuck to his forearms.

BACK AT THE hospital early in the morning, Joe sees Pop awake for the first time in days. The breathing tube is out and all the IV's. Pop's sitting on the side of his bed, feet dangling just above the terrazzo floor. He seems to be contemplating his toes. He looks just like he did the weeks following Mom's death, fighting depression, not eating, hoping to die. Doesn't notice Joe watching him. Reminds Joe of the dog he had once that got lost and was found weeks later at the pound hours before the putdown. Joe doesn't get a word in before Pop stretches out his hand and motions him over, checking the door for Keys.

"They say I'm gettin' out," he says in a sore raspy voice. "That true? 'Cause if it's not, I'm leavin' anyway, boy. Not gonna be another notch on that bastard's belt like the rest of 'em. Where's my pants?"

"What bastard?"

Pop grabs Joe's arm like a life preserver and pulls him close. "*Keys.*"

86

"Dude with claws?"

"You felt 'em, too?" Pop points down the ward, "See all these empty beds?"

"You're the last to go. So?"

"Not the last to go. I stay here another night and I'll be resting next to Mom. They didn't leave, *Who-Ass*. He killed 'em!" Pop's eyes glisten in the dull light of the empty ward.

Joe feels Pop's desperation, knows he's telling the truth. "What's going on?"

Pop grabs Joe's shoulder and pulls him closer. "Comes in at night and gives 'em a shot. They die and he wheels 'em out. Knocked me out a couple a times so I wouldn't see anything, but Mick clued me in. Then old Cecil calls me over one night and tells me were all gonna die. He's dead the next day. And the penicillin I got? No accident. Keys pulls out the hypo and hits me in the thigh with it. See here," Pop pulls up his gown and shows Joe the puncture mark haloed by a light bruise. "Wasn't no mix up. Did it on purpose 'cause I told the nurse he was up to no good and I was gonna to tell the doc."

Joe stands up straight and rubs Pop's back. "It's okay, Pop."

"Don't believe me, do you?"

"I believe you. We can't do nothin' about it now. Let's get you outa here." Joe checks the closet, pulls out Pop's street clothes and hands him his pants. He collects the rest of his belongings in the overnight bag and crams dirties into a plastic grocery bag.

"Not leaving me here are you, I mean while you sign them papers and what not?"

"No, Pop, you're coming with me."

As they head for the door, Pop grabs Joe's arm and stops. He looks down the empty ward. "Just old guys like me. Didn't deserve it. They fought for the country and this crap's how they get repaid."

The drive home is quiet, Joe resting his arm on the window and rubbing at his temple, Pop staring out at the distance dreaming things up in his head. No one wants conversation. Neither wants the responsibility of broaching a threat of action.

Pop's ready to be back in his own bed. Might, he thinks, stay in it for days. Joe's silence is disconcerting, much like the imminent eruption of a volcano. It feels foreign to Pop, a side of Joe he's never seen before. So much so, he turns on the radio just to breathe.

"Storm in the Atlantic turned to a hurricane," Joe comments.

"What storm's that?"

"Forget the name. They're thinkin' it might come here." Joe stops at the red light and taps the volume button. Announcer gives a blow by blow of the latest coordinates and reminds listeners they might want to stock up before the big rush.

"Guess we'll do some shopping tomorrow before it's all gone," Joe says, rolling through the green light.

13

black eyed hurricane

LOWE'S, DOESN'T SEEM so bad as long as you don't need lumber. The remaining plywood lies split and in pieces piled in the corner, but by closing even those will be seized, the upper shelves stripped clean. Maglites and batteries are good movers, so are those blue tarps that after last year's storms still grace many a roof.

Joe drifts up and down the aisles hunting for last minute bargains while keeping a close eye on the double pack D cell batteries in his cart, knows all he has to do is turn his back for a second and they'll be swiped. Can't help but notice what some other folks bought: ceiling fans, freezers, useless things that take up space when the power goes out. Folks new to hurricane season.

Joe's made sure Pop's pantry is full of dry goods, not for storm preparedness, but because he hates going to the grocery and doesn't trust Pop in the kitchen anymore. Joe isn't what you'd call a gourmet cook, but he can open a can and heat it on the stove. In the event of a hurricane, their life style won't change much.

Standing in line for checkout, Joe notices a young woman standing in front of him, on her hip, a cranky two-year-old wearing nothing but a wet diaper. Betty, a good ten years ago. A butterfly tattoo infests the small of the young mother's back. The curvature of her back makes the butterfly wings appear to be moving. Joe admires the crisp detailed colors.

His gut knots. He's been afraid to talk to her ever since Ricky moved back, but an instinct blaring in his gut tells him that something's wrong and it urges him to decide to roll by her place on the way home, maybe knock on the door, see how's she's doing. His heart pounds just thinking about it, starts reciting in his head what to say to Ricky if pinned down again, misses the question from the clerk about if he's found everything he needs. He nods, digs out two twenties from the leather bag suspended from his belt and quickly slides out the automatic doors without collecting his change.

Every gas station passed has yellow bags over the nozzles, but still carry lots of beer and cigarettes. Stations that have gas tempt vehicles lined bumper to bumper all the way around the block. A fist fight breaks out at the BP on Bay Street as he goes by. A big guy takes one to the mouth and goes down.

Most buildings are boarded, some with expensive billboard signs suspiciously abstracted from their usual sites. City workers stack sandbags to divert the predicted deluge of water from the streets. Shelters fill up. Mobile home parks empty.

Joe cruises past Betty's apartment, slows to a crawl, takes in as much information from the looks of the place as he can. Her car's gone. A few half-rotten two by fours are nailed across the frames of the windows, but nothing to protect them from the flying sheets of aluminum or remaining commercial signage torn and given flight in high winds. Tells himself she's with a friend. Or maybe Ricky's taken her to a sturdier shelter or motel room. Joe drives home depressed.

Back at the house, Joe boards up windows and pulls lawn furniture into the garage. There's nothing to secure other than the shed and it doesn't need much.

Joe sees Dee Dee has stacked her lawn furniture against the house as if the wind will be respectful and leave it there. He thinks of saying something to her but decides against it, knowing it will only give her another opportunity to go off on him about the dog.

DEE DEE DOESN'T bother to board up, hates sitting in the dark in a lonely house listening to the wind and rain beating against it. She prefers to stand at the window and watch things fly by.

She's mesmerized watching Joe through nicotine dimmed window curtains, talking under her breath as if he can hear her, wishing the big oak in the yard would fall on him. Watch him suffer a slow death.

Cigarette smoke curls past her tear swollen face, the Virginia Slim burning close to the filter between her stubby fingers. She's bitten off her otherwise perfect custom manicured nails done by that Asian girl who painted a nice design on each, nails she'd patiently cared for until they grew long and arched; the envy of all the women at her church. She'd not bothered to call for a return appointment. Her kinky hair falls loose against her shoulders, unmanaged for almost a week, unthinkable for a black woman. She's lost the will to bathe regularly and hasn't left the house in over five days.

Housekeeping falls in line after personal hygiene. Soured dirty dishes sit stacked in the kitchen and on the nightstand by her unmade bed. Clothes once treasured lie on the floor throughout the house. Food rots in the dog's bowl by the kitchen sink, now a smorgasbord for cockroaches once periodically poisoned or beaten to death with the dish towel. The thought of washing the bowl is the same as admitting she's given up.

Wind howls around the north side of the house, scraping shrubs against the front window. She flops in the recliner, lights another cigarette, and waits for the storm.

THE FIRST HEAVY feeder bands blow through just after seven in the evening, brushing the crepe myrtles aside like a tipsy bar fly, and stripping the colorful blooms from their stalks. Red, pink, and white petals litter the air like confetti, spattering in the street from the downpour. Rain begins to fall in thick sheets.

Pop drinks black coffee at the kitchen table, wearing nothing but shorts, socks, and slippers. Joe sets up battery powered lights in kitchen, hallway, bathroom—anywhere he and Pop might need to go.

A pot of stew bubbles on the stove while there's still power, and Joe's brought in the propane camp stove and a large plastic cooler stocked with beer, sodas, water, and ice.

"Got enough ice there?" Pop asks, stretches his neck to see but doesn't care enough to inspect.

"Got more in the big freezer in the shed," Joe says. Sets extra towels by the back door then stirs the stew.

"What freezer you talkin' about?"

"One I picked up while you were in the place. Not much to look at, but it freezes things all right."

"What'll you store in there?" Pop starts to get up with his cup and Joe waves him back down, takes the cup and pours him a refill.

"Mostly ice right now. Thought after all this we might get some meat. Save some money. Take advantage of specials. The way mom did, remember?"

Pop doesn't answer and the silence makes Joe feel he shouldn't have mentioned her. He takes two bowls from the cabinet, ladles in stew, and sets them on the table with a loaf of bread. Pop starts on the stew before Joe sits down, shoveling it in like a starving vagrant. Stops Joe in his tracks. Realizes the old guy probably hasn't eaten a real meal since before the attack.

Violent wind shakes loose a section of aluminum soffit.

"Just how bad was it in there, Pop?" Joe pulls a slice of bread from the wrapper and sops it in stew gravy, hopes the question doesn't shut Pop down and send him to his room.

"Liked to make 'em suffer. Did mean things and was glad about it." Pop reaches for the bread. Joe takes a slice out and hands it to him.

"No need to explain if it's hard."

"Explain! Bastard slit Frank like a piece of meat," Pop drops his spoon in the bowl, slaps his hands on the table, "should a seen him, JoJo. Layin' out for anyone to see. No dignity, bleedin' like a school girl. Keys makin' sure we all know he's boss by what he done to Frank."

"What about the rest of 'em?"

Shoving meat around the bowl, Pop takes a deep breath, "Sammy went next. Quit askin' who everybody was, remember? Started to sleep a lot. I thought I was havin' a dream. I see Keys standing over his bed late one night, stickin' him with something. Next day he's gone, too."

Joe squeezes his spoon until his knuckles turn white.

"Teases Cecil with a fat dessert, you know, one of those strawberry...what do you call 'em?"

"Shortcakes?"

"That's right. Holds it under Cecil's nose until life comes back to his eyes then pulls it away, Cecil knowin' he ain't gettin' any. Makes him beg for it. Eats it in front of him." Pop stabs the hunk of beef, but can't bring himself to put it in his mouth. "Cecil calls me over and whispers, 'We're all gonna die.' I know in my gut he's telling the truth. I can see in Mick's eyes he knows it, too."

"How soon they get taken out of the room after what Keys does?"

"That night. Gives me something to knock me out. Then it's Mick's turn. He comes back from some procedure on his lungs. He's a lot a trouble to Keys that night. Keys has to come in and out a lot to care for him and it pisses him off. When it got late, Keys takes off Mick's mask, turns off his machine, and holds him down until he quits breathin'."

Joe wants more, searches Pop's face for a signal he can go on. "He just gives you the shot?"

Pop opens his mouth just as the power flickers. "Just? Is him squeezin' my tore up arm, or stickin' a needle in the raw meat enough? Is him leanin' over telling me to keep my mouth shut or else, enough?" Pop holds Joe's gaze.

The soffit tears from the roof and sails into darkness.

"It's enough." Joe pushes his bowl aside, stands by the back door watching the storm through the only window not boarded up. Rain pelts the painted steel sheathing like a pressure washer. Joe sees water filling the back yard as a small river expands dumping excess water down into the pond.

"Don't mean to get you upset. Think I'll check the weather. Don't think it's gonna be more than a category one." Joe goes to the phone in the living room before the lines die and dials a number.

Pop's unsettled, unsure if it's the storm or his experiences at the place. Collecting dishes, he washes up and puts things away. Feels safe now with Joe in the house.

BY ELEVEN THIRTY, the eye of the hurricane is moving over the area.

Joe slips out of his bedroom to check on Pop. He's asleep in front of Marilyn Monroe, the TV going snowy, then clearing out again as the hurricane's eye wall moves out. Pop's top denture has lost its adhesiveness and settled on his bottom denture, saliva attached like puppet strings. A shot that would be the envy of any cheap horror movie director.

They still have power, but the surges leave the clocks and VCR flashing twelve o'clock. Joe picks up the big yellow flashlight on Pop's side table and flicks it on and off. Sets it back. He checks Pop's pill bottle then checks his watch, relieved Pop has taken his medication without having to be reminded. The threat of having to go back to the hospital seems like good incentive to take it regularly. Probably never get the old guy back there no matter how bad hurt or sick, and then what? Watch him waste away from something as simple as a head cold turned infectious? Then he'd die and leave a legal mess, questions of why didn't he get him medical treatment, neglect allegations with TV coverage of the bad son who let his poor old man suffer.

Pulling a raincoat from the hall closet, Joe slips out the front door.

14

what dead guy?

SITTING ACROSS FROM the hospital, Joe watches the employee exit in a light rain with the car window rolled down, gnawing on his thumb nail. Chews off a hanging cuticle and spits it out the window, watching medical employees sprint to their cars after shift, leaving while the gettin' is good.

Five minutes later, Keys exits, pulls his lab coat over his head and swaggers towards his truck. Joe meets him halfway, the hood of his rain jacket pulled down. Eyes shifting for potential witnesses, Joe steps up, "Hey buddy, can you help me?" Points to his car. "My wife's having a baby. Don't think she'll make it inside. Can you help me out?"

Keys shoots him a suspicious glance. "Now? She can't make it on her own?"

"No man. I think the baby's crowning." Joe pulls Keys by the sleeve to the car.

"Going to have a hurricane baby," Keys jokes, walks around to the passenger door. The eye of the storm is passing quickly. Heavy rain roars through the alley behind them. Wind howls around the buildings blowing the bottom of Joe's raincoat up to the waist, soaking the bottom of his shorts. He opens the car door and steps back.

Keys leans in, "Hey, where's your wife?"

Joe figures the angle, cocks both arms far above his head and slams Keys' head into the door post so hard it knocks him out cold. Shoves Keys into the passenger seat and shuts the door.

Rain stings Joe's face, snaps against his raincoat. His heart pounds. Inside the car, Joe pushes his hood back, takes a moment to pull himself together. Glances at Keys slumped into the dash, wonders how much time he has until he comes-to. He pushes Keys back against the seat and belts him in, inspects the crushed, thin bone of the temple imbedded in Keys' brain. Doesn't look so good. He feels Keys' neck for a pulse. Presses a little harder. Nothing.

"Shit!"

Joe's hands start trembling around the steering wheel, semi-frozen, tries to think. Slings the car door open, leans out holding the steering wheel, and pukes in the rain. Cold rain pelts the back of his head dowsing the urge to flee the car, to pretend this isn't happening. He pulls himself back up, closes the door and sits next to dead man Keys with no sound in the car but the rain beating on oxidized paint over old metal.

"Weren't supposed to *die!*" Joe yells, sticks his finger in Keys' face, "You weren't supposed to *die!*"

He can't sit here worrying, knows someone will call the cops, find out he's killed a guy. He shoves Keys against the window and pulls out into the water swollen street. "Just supposed to scare you," Joe mumbles.

On the corner of Kurt Street and Ardice, the street light is out, swinging precariously from one line as if waiting to pounce on some unsuspecting motorist. Joe eases through, but hits the brakes to avoid a newspaper box scuttling across the road, forcing the car to slide into a veterinary sign.

Joe sits with both hands braced against the steering wheel, blood drained from his face. He takes a deep breath, drops the transmission into reverse. The rearview mirror illuminates his face in a blue strobe.

It's a rooky cop cruising the streets for debris blocking the roadway, looters scouting for a windfall, or folks trapped in damaged mobile homes, or stalled vehicles. Despite the storm, so far all he's come up on are branches and thrill-seeking tourists out to experience the storm up close and personal. Taps on Joe's car window with a Maglite.

Shit. Joe flushes, glances at Keys and reluctantly rolls the window down a few inches. "Officer?"

Too young to be a real cop. Joe thinks it might be a high school student perpetrating a senior practical joke. Doesn't think they'd carry real guns, though. Gun looks real. Probably a real cop then, too.

Cop yells over the wind, "Sir, you all right? See you've got a problem." Peers quizzically through the window. Maglite beam fills the interior. Stops on Keys.

"We're okay, Officer. Dodged, dodged, dodged somethin' rollin' across the road here and slid into the sign," Joe stutters, his knuckles locked around the steering wheel, inhaling the cop's onion breath.

"Your friend okay? Got an ugly bump on his head."

"Drunk. Got drunk. Yeah, picked a fight with the wrong guy at one of those hurricane parties. Broke up with his girlfriend." Joe forces a laugh. "Called, called me to pick him up and take him home. See, he'll be fine once I get him home. To bed, see." Pats Keys on the shoulder, glad he put the dead guy in a seatbelt.

"Know there's a curfew, right?"

Maglite sweeps the backseat, settles on Keys again. Rain comes in sideways, blowing the cop's yellow rain slicker up. The hood fills with air and pushes it off his head.

"Sorry, Officer. I'm almost home. Any damage to the sign?" *Please, please, please leave.*

Cop goes to the front of the car, scans the sign and Joe's bumper with the flashlight. Joe briefly weighs the possibilities of running him over while watching the cop's light beam trying to penetrate the heavy rain.

Cop sloshes back to the window struggling to hold the hood over his head with one hand and yells, "You got lucky. Just pushed the sign back. No break." A wind gust strips the hood off again.

Soaked, the cop starts shivering.

"Am I free to go? Got to get the dead man home," Joe yells, rain pelting his face from the crack in the window.

"You say dead man?" Cop asks, watching Joe's lips.

"Did I?" *Shit!* "Yeah, he'll be a dead man when his wife finds out."

"Thought you said he just broke up with his girlfriend?"

"Now you know why he's a dead man!" Joe yells back, grinning.

"You sure he's okay?" Cop settles the light back on Keys again.

"Really plowed this time. Out cold and just as well if you know what I mean."

"I hear that. You drive safe." Cop tips his chin and hurries back to his dry patrol car.

Joe reverses and crawls back onto the road. Drives twenty miles an hour in the rain pouring so hard he can barely see two feet past the hood. Uses the center reflectors in the road to guide him home.

15

strike a pose

IN THE DRIVEWAY, Joe chews another fingernail while staring at Keys. Reaches over and smacks Keys on the head. "*Asshole!*" Taps the steering wheel. "What now? Dump you on the side of the road?"

Joe watches the windshield wipers flicking back and forth. "*Damn it!*" Smacks him again.

He turns off the engine, pulls the keys from the ignition, and selects the key to the shed.

IT'S HARD FOR Dee Dee to see who's inside the car with her nose pressed against the living room window. She can barely make out through the downpour, just before the street light goes out, what appears to be two people, wonders who Joe's dragged home in the middle of a hurricane. Never seen anyone at the house other than the white trash spick chick that drove Pop home. Maybe the spicks got the dog. Maybe she saw it one

100

day and decided she liked it and the two of them planned a way to lure it out and snatch it.

The tip of her cigarette smolders against the rain-pelted glass as she watches Joe cower out of the car, open the passenger door, and drag Keys into the pouring rain.
Joe struggles with the body. It slips through his arms. Aggravated and out of breath, Joe kicks Keys in the ribs. Grabs Key's collar and tries dragging him again, slips in the mud and slides under the body. He shoves Keys' shoulder and flips him over, crawls to his feet, grabs Keys under the arms, and drags him to the gate.

Dee Dee's lips part. Her fingers slowly touch the glass. She bolts from the living room and runs through the dark house. Slams her knee against the bedroom door and hobbles to the window that looks out at the Salas's side yard.

JOE DROPS KEYS in the mud again, opens the gate, heaves Keys up and drags him across the backyard to the shed.

Dee Dee shoves herself from the window and runs down the dark hallway to the kitchen. Slams right into the table. The table jams into the sheetrock, knocking stacks of empty jars, glasses, and Cheez-Its boxes to the floor. A chair flips on its side. She trips over the chair and spills across the worn linoleum. Doesn't think she's broken anything, lies there long enough to catch her breath then crawls across the floor to the sliding glass door.

She slides the door open and steps out on the patio. Water cascades from the roof valley like a fire hose, taking her breath away and turning her dyed hair into flat red ropes. Two steps off the patio, Dee Dee bolts across the soggy yard, mud and grass squishing between her toes, takes too long a stride and slips. She water-slides to a stop three feet from the fence line. Rolling over, she crawls on her hands and knees, driving rain stinging her eyes, the wind tearing at her thin cotton muu muu.

She's suddenly aware how close she is to the shed and puts her shaky hand to her mouth. Peers with one wet blinking eye between the slats.

JOE DROPS KEYS in the mud and unlocks the shed. The wind rips the shed door from his hand and pins it against the wall. He drags Keys in by the arm and lays him out across the concrete floor while rain drains from the body and puddles to the low spot at the back of the shed.

Joe finds his flashlight and uses it to locate the propane lantern. Its anemic glow fills the shed, leaves the surrounding walls in sharp-edged shadows. The flashlight beam sweeps along the fence as Joe fights the door closed.

DEE DEE JUMPS from the light, lands in a small stream cut into the yard by the rain. Pulling herself up, she clutches the fence for support in the 45-miles-per-hour wind, steps through the mushy yard and is through her back gate before Joe can throw the lock on the shed door.

"WHAT DO YOU think? Not fancy, but I've got a lot of good stuff," Joe says to Keys. Hangs his raincoat on a nail by the door. Wind-driven rain hammers the worn boards in waves.

"At least it's a place to stay," Joe says, "until I think of where to dump you." Joe sets the lantern on the bench next to his art supplies. Strips two paper towels from the roll, wipes his face and stares down at Keys draining on the floor, mulling over how to get rid of him.

In the faint glow of the lantern, the curvature of Keys' bone structure stands out, softens along the cheek, becomes defined at the nose and brow line. Keys is no longer Keys, but to the eye of an artist, a possibility. In Joe's imagination, the face is that of a model, reliable, cooperative. He admires the raw beauty of it, kneels so he can follow the bone structure with his finger, pressing the cheek, the edge of the lip, the ear.

Joe reads over notes thumbtacked to the pegboard. Recites twice so he doesn't forget the process. Right off there's a problem. Keys is bigger than a fish. Could take the machete hanging on the wall and cut his head off, but doesn't want to deal with all the blood. Always a lot of blood in the movies. Could try to shelve Keys on the bench, strap him to the wall with tie downs. Thinks that's a workable solution.

In minutes, he's cleared the counter, installed tie downs to the back wall with anchor bolts. He lifts Keys by the shoulders and drags him over to the bench.

Joe hoists Keys under the arms, considers his fixed eyes, his slackened mouth. Keys' cold face presses to his cheek as he heaves the body to the edge of the bench. Grossed, he loses his grip and the body pitches forward to the floor. Keys' face scuds across the concrete, scraping the skin off the left side. Joe kicks Keys in the gut. "*Idiot!*"

Keys' arms, stiffening from the onset of rigor, extend from the body like a mannequin's. Pisses Joe off and he kicks Keys in the gut again. Feels a little better. He sits the body upright against the bench, takes the lantern and holds it to Keys' face. No damage to the right profile from what Joe can make out.

DEE DEE CREEPS along the fence line shivering. She briefly considers going back home, but curiosity insists she move on. Rain pours off the tip of her nose and stings her eyes. Her thick hand contacts the worn wood on the side of the shed, searching for a crack of light, a passage into Joe's secret. She presses her ear to the board, hears muffled conversation. Thinks there might be a fight, can't hear much in the howling wind. The back of her muu muu catches on rose thorns and shreds. Exposes her ass swaddled inadequately in a twisted thong that she tugs at it with one hand.

JOE PULLS THE instructions off the board and sits on the floor next to Keys. Holds the towel to the lamp and reads through the "Making a Print" section.

"To guarantee good printing results, it's useful to understand fish anatomy," Joe reads aloud to Keys. "Review anatomy with students. 'Well, children, what we have here is *not* covered in the instructions."

Joe sizes Keys up and reads on. "It says here, Keys, to plug the anus with a small paper wad to insure it won't leak onto your printing paper." Joe smiles, flips the towel over. "Place on newspaper covered table. That didn't work out so well. Let's use the floor."

Joe sets the towel down, reaches under the bench for a stack of old newspapers and spreads them across the floor. Grabs Keys' jacket and lowers him flat on the floor, stiff knees in the air.

Joe reads on, squinting at his barely legible handwriting. "Brush a thin coat of ink using a one-half inch brush. Think I'll use a two inch. Wait, it says to clean the surface first with soap and water to remove dirt and mucus, then dry well." Joe takes the lantern and holds it to Keys' muddy face.

DEE DEE CREEPS to the shed door and places her hand on the knob. At that precise moment, a sizzling bolt of lightning instantly followed by a clap of thunder, clouts the backyard. And slapping her hand to her mouth, she shrieks.

Joe drops the lantern, throws a tarp over the body and goes to the door, sees Dee Dee scuttling along the fence line. He can just make out the two lunar cheeks of her ass jogging up and down as her stubby legs hustle towards the gate.

"What are you doing!" he yells, sprinting across the yard. "What do you want?" He grabs her thick shoulder and spins her around. "You spying on me?"

Dee Dee shrieks, "Nothing! Leave me alone." She twists toward the gate.

"You nosey bitch." Joe, astounded at the feeling of power he's gotten from killing, grabs her shoulder again, "Keep out of my business if you don't want to end up like your dog!"

Dee Dee covers her mouth in horror, slogs through the gate, down the side yard, through her gate, and into her own back yard. She leans against the stucco wall out of breath, hand to her stomach. Sidles into her dark house. Locking herself in, she stands shivering by the sliding glass door afraid to peer out.

BACK AT THE shed, Joe thinks about options. He doesn't think Dee Dee knows about Keys, but knows she might tell the cops what she suspects if she saw him dragging him to the shed. Did that with the dog.

Power's still out, and the phone, so that gives him time. Won't have the luxury now of dragging Keys back to the car and dropping him off somewhere far, figures he has a few hours to complete this project before the storm moves past.

He takes a small paint bucket and washes the dried mud from Keys' face, then blots it dry with paper towels. Just like the instructions say. He separates a sheet of moisture-tolerant paper from the roll and sets it on the floor next to a small pan of permanent India ink and a two-inch brush. Getting in a comfortable position, Joe takes the brush, dips it in the ink and coats the entire right side of Keys' face. Presses the paper into the ink, pats it, presses harder. Feels around like a blind man reading a face, then pulls the paper off and inspects the result.

Not exactly human. It's a black inky blob with a faint image of… what? Joe can't tell. A miserable failure is what it is.

He explodes, shredding the paper, leans against the leg of the bench with his arm across his face. Black ink smears his arms and chin like an emerging coal miner's. Joe sits quiet and reads the instructions one more time. He pulls another sheet of paper from the roll and re-inks Keys' face. "Take your time, there, JoJo. Enjoy the process."

An hour into it and the prints become progressively better. Four of them lie scattered on the concrete floor, each one with better detail than the last. Gives Joe the hope and confidence he desperately needs to keep trying.

"Ever wonder what you'd look like as a black man?" he asks Keys. "Now here comes the tricky part. Don't move."

Joe places the bottom edge of the paper under Keys' chin then carefully finger rolls the paper inch by inch, pressing gently all the way to the forehead. Smoothes and presses across the cheek, the indent by the nose, eye socket, the eyebrow.

"Be careful not to wrinkle or move paper excessively, the instructions say," Joe mutters, sticking a straight pin through the paper and into Keys' scalp to hold it in place. Sticks pins into the paper behind the ear. One in the neck.

"Now, buddy, time for the fine detail work," Joe says, hunched over inches from the paper. "You're going to be famous. Too bad you're too dead to enjoy it."

Joe feels for the lips and gently indents with a capped ink pen. Moves onto the eye socket. "On a fish I'm supposed to leave it blank and paint it in myself, but I think your eyes are great. With luck I might be able to pick up the lashes."

Joe pulls the pin from the top of the scalp and gently pulls the paper down to inspect his work. He's elated. Pressed into the paper are premature crows' feet, hair from the brow and hairline, even fine lines from the lips. He quickly unpins the rest and holds the print up to the light.

He chews on his ragged thumbnail and smiles. Acne scars, the indent around the temple, all there. The effect of flattening the curved face is somehow sidelong and adds an aspect both lifelike and mysteriously askew.

Joe leans against the bench, the print on his lap, and laughs. "Thanks, Keys. Sorry about the accident." He pins the sheet to the pegboard to dry and steps back against the door.

It's even better from across the room.

Wind speed downgrades to 20-mph gusts interspersed with lengthening periods of calm. Power lines hang loose from snapped tree limbs, but the power company trucks are already moving into neighborhoods to reconnect.

What to do with the body? Joe sees the box of black garbage bags on the floor and smiles, opens the shed door and looks through the fence to be sure Dee Dee isn't crouching on the other side. He rolls Keys in the tarp and drags him out of the shed to the gate that leads to the pond. One quick glance back and Joe drags the body through the brush to the dead pine.

Water's risen two feet higher than before the storm, the mud now a mucky adhesive that threatens to suck the shoes off his feet. Joe huffs out of breath dragging the body to the edge of the woods so it can't be seen from the house.

Daylight's just breaking through the swirling outer feeder bands. A small downed water oak lies partially submerged in the pond. Somehow the dead pine is no worse for wear.

Joe spreads out the tarp and strips the clothing from Keys' body. He retrieves the wallet from the pants and slides out the cash. Counts it. One hundred and twenty dollars and a condom. Rolls Keys off the tarp, his pale skin glistening under the black ink like some anointed pagan sacrifice.

Joe feels sad. Not because Keys is dead, but because he's chanced to be the first immortalized. Joe knows it. He's grateful for the resurrection of his dying art career and even more grateful that Keys is dead. Payment in full for what he did to his father and all the other old guys.

He gathers the clothes, wallet, tarp, and walks home whistling in a drizzling rain. All and all, he thinks, it's been a good night.

16

clothing optional

POP LIMPS THROUGH the house to check on Joe. Pushes Joe's bedroom door ajar and sees he's laid sideways on the bed asleep. Pop thinks a breakfast would be good and suddenly the power comes on. He can't help clapping—wouldn't in front of other people—limps to the kitchen in nothing but his underwear.

Air handler drones in the hall closet working overtime to cool the house from the ninety-degree temperatures.

Joe smells bacon. Hell of a dream, he thinks. Rolls over and realizes he's still in street clothes; socks, dirty and stiff, still stuck to his feet. His tee shirt's smeared with mud. Everything stinks. He stinks. Sniffs his pits and that's all that's needed to wake him up.

Checking his watch, he knows he's slept a good four hours, wants to shut his eyes and go back to sleep, but it's too late. His mind begins to review the last twelve hours like a newsreel he can't shut off, then he smells bacon and knows Pop's in the kitchen cookin' without supervision.

Pop's draining bacon on paper towels wearing nothing but an apron over his underwear to catch hot grease splatter when Joe comes in.

"There's a picture for you," he mutters to himself, sees Pop's underwear sagging in the ass all stretched out. Thinks there can't be much elasticity there anymore and makes a mental note to pick up a new set for him at the Wal-Mart.

A carton of eggs waits for the bacon to move on, and coffee perks away in the pot. Kitchen's been cleaned up, dishes put away, and the cooler's empty, waiting by the back door.

Pop notices Joe standing there watching him. "Got breakfast goin' here. Cookin' up this bacon 'fore it goes bad. Know I'm not supposed to be cookin' but woke hungry enough to eat the ass-end out of a boar hog. Didn't want to bother you none. You hungry?"

"Not so much," Joe mumbles, wipes his eyes, gets a whiff of his stink again. "Gonna shower. Won't take long. Don't burn the house down while I'm in it."

"I'll burn it while you're out," Pop grins without teeth. Notices Joe's condition for the first time. "What happened there? Look like you were in one of them mud wrestling contests," he says pulling the last slice out of the pan with a fork.

"Had to go out and secure stuff around the house last night. Real mess out there."

"You look worse. Never could keep you clean. Dirty little kid you were," Pop says. Cracks two eggs in the pan and fishes shells out of the goo.

Joe rolls his eyes and heads for the shower.

DEE DEE'S PLOPPED down in the recliner wearing nothing but her thong, mud caked to her feet and ankles, watching the Salas's driveway. She's stripped off the shredded muu muu that's now bunched in the middle of the kitchen floor, an added layer for the massing cockroaches.

She's checked the phone a dozen times before it finally connects. Calls 911 the second there's a dial tone. Okay, so the dispatcher thinks it's a crank call and hangs up on her. Twice. On the third try he promises to send a unit as soon as one's available, but says it might be a while. He hangs up on her in the middle of her shriek of indignation for being dismissed like a child. She yells into the phone that she is not gonna to leave the house without a police escort. "You hear me?" she insists. "There's a dead man in my neighbor's shed and blood's everywhere. Kilt my dog, too!"

She moves from the living room to the kitchen, sucking warm Dr. Pepper from the can and finishing off a bag of stale chips. Tips the bag above her mouth, gives it a shake. Salty crumbs that miss her mouth litter the top of her heavy breasts like confetti. She opens the back door, wads up the bag and pitches it into the backyard.

Her backyard's a wreck. Lawn furniture's pinned against the back fence, half buried in mud. Torrents of water that spewed off the roof like Niagara gouged trenches through the lawn. The downspout separated from the gutter, creating a pit at the corner of the foundation. Nothing remains of the begonia beds. Only thing standing upright is the creepy garden gnome.

The concrete patio's is as far as Dee Dee will venture, nudity not even part of the equation, doesn't dare move close to the fence as if some invisible hand will reach over and snatch her out of the yard and into the hands of her murderous neighbor. She listens intently for any sound from the shed.

Can't think of food, or cleaning herself up, afraid showering will cause her to miss something crucial.

Dee Dee sits in a kitchen chair in the doorway to the backyard, smoking. Flicks the filter into the yard, waiting for the cops.

JOE'S REFRESHED. Put on clean clothes. Shaved. Trimmed his nails.

Pop's dressed, too. A crisp white short-sleeve shirt, trousers pulled up to his tits, held on with a belt so old the holes have in-between splits. A present from Mom. One of those Father's Day gifts. She'd bought everything he owns. He'd thought about venturing out to buy new, but realized she knew where to go, what size. With him being colorblind, she did all the matching, too. Sure, he could manage if he had to. Seems better to wait until the old stuff wore out and fell apart. Won't be long from the looks of most of it.

He's sewn up the ass of the trousers he has on with the sewing kit found in the bathroom, and all in all it has worked well enough if you didn't notice the fabric bunching on the right side. Made the right leg a little tight, but his ass doesn't hang out for the world to see.

Passing through the living room, Joe sees Pop staring out the front window.

"Whatcha doin', Pop?"

"Cops at Dee Dee's place. Why you suppose that is?" Pop asks.

Joe stands next to him, watches the two cops unfold from their marked units and walk up to Dee Dee's front door. Joe flushes. Rolls his eyes.

"What's wrong, JoJo?"

"Haven't a clue, Pop. You say there's breakfast warm in the kitchen still?"

"Coffee, too. Take you an aspirin there while you're at it. You're flushed. Maybe caught somethin' out in the weather last night. Can't afford both of us being sick. One of us is plenty." Pop leans closer to the window, ignores Joe.

"You take your pill today?"

"Yes, I took my pill," Pop says, annoyed he's reminded like a child.

Joe's half-way through breakfast when the doorbell rings. Heart rate kicks up a notch. Before leaving for the living room, he looks out the window to the pond. Sunlight glistens on the calm water.

"JoJo, cops here!" Pop yells from the front door.

They stand filling the doorway. Two of them big as linebackers, heads shaved, sunglasses hooked to the epaulets on their shoulders, geared for war. They bend down to get through the doorway. Portable radios chatter in code from their belts. Cop One presses the mic on his shoulder and answers back. Numbers mostly. He doesn't appear to be spooked by anything yet.

"Joe Salas. This is my father, Anthony." Joe shakes Cop One's hand. "Anything wrong, Officers?"

"Received a complaint from a Dee Dee Turner. Your neighbor."

Cop Two separates from Cop One and starts evaluating Joe, the old man, the stuff in the room. Stands with his forearm resting on the butt of his holstered semiautomatic, thumb tucked into his duty belt, eyes roaming as if fugitives might scramble from the woodwork.

"What complaint?" Joe asks, sitting on the edge of the sofa with his arms crossed over his chest.

"Won't be the first time, can tell you that," Pop interrupts, both hands on his hips, scowls up into Cop One's face, dwarfed by his size. Doesn't seem intimidated in the least. Joe can't help but smile.

"Been a snobby busybody ever since she moved in. Makin' up shit," Pop bitches, "and it's not 'cause she's black, either. She makes up shit."

"Pop, why don't you finish the kitchen?"

Pop gives Joe a good stare down. Quick limps away because now he's mad for being dismissed like a hysterical female.

"Sorry about that. He's old. Says whatever. What she complainin' about now?" Joe asks.

Cop One pulls a notebook from his belt and flips a page. "What did she complain about before?" Watches Joe's expression when he answers.

"Thinks I got rid of her dog."

"Did you?" Cop watches closer like he's worming his way into Joe's brain.

"Like I told the Animal Control Officer, I've only lived here a few weeks. Don't really know the woman. Couldn't tell you why she's all over us. Animal Control said the dog dug out and that was the end of it. She back on it again?"

"Not exactly. Got a shed out back, Mr. Salas?"

"Got a shed. Animal Control checked it," Joe says chewing his thumb nail.

"Mind if we check it out?"

"No, not at all. We can go through the kitchen here." Joe leads them through the house, feels their presence like a deep chill.

Pop trails loosely behind. Doesn't want to miss anything.

Joe unlocks the shed and flips on the light, swings the door against the wall to hide the print of Keys' face hung drying on the back of it.

Cop Two enters and stands in the middle of the room, takes his time to survey the contents and condition. He takes special note of the concrete floor and tools on the peg board.

114

Joe stares at the ground, mildly pissed, turns and sees Dee Dee through the fence perched on her patio straining to view what's going on. Shakes his head, sees the cop's watching him.

"This is getting old," Joe complains.

Cop Two picks up the machete and holds the edge of the blade up to the light. He sets it back on the peg board and notices the freezer. "What do you keep in here?"

"Nothing right now. Kept ice before the storm," Joe says.

Cop Two opens the freezer, takes a small Maglite from his duty belt and shines it around the inside. Closes it. "Anyone in here lately?"

Joe looks at Pop. "No. Just the Animal Control Officer."

Cop Two picks around on the bench, notices the paints and artist brushes. "You an artist?" Takes time to read the instructions on the paper towel hanging on the peg board.

"Some say yes, some no."

Cop turns, "Which is it?"

"Waiting for discovery. Not much inspiration lately." Briefly glances at Pop, embarrassed he's baring his deepest dreams and disappointments. Remembers all the sports stuff he's dragged out of the shed and sent to the landfill.

Cop One tilts his head at Cop Two. Cop Two slides past Joe to the back yard. He wanders the fence line pressing the ground with full weight on his boot searching for soft impressions in the yard that might be a hastily dug burial site.

Cop One leaves the shed, keys the mic, and calls into dispatch.

Joe shrugs at Pop.

"Just need a few things for my report, Mr. Salas," Cop One tells him, signals for Cop Two to break off and go to the car.

Joe follows them through the gate and up the side yard to the front.

Cop Two goes to the patrol car, opens the trunk, retrieves paperwork, and walks up to Dee Dee's front door. She's out on the front porch before his foot hits the top step, wearing nothing but a robe. Mud, white against her dark skin, streaks her feet and calves.

Joe can't hear what he's telling her, tries to listen in-between answering questions from Cop One for his offence incident report. Full name, address, birth date, phone number.

Dee Dee explodes on Cop Two, has her finger jammed in his chest screaming obscenities.

Cop One slips the pen in the report pad in his hand and lets it drop to his side.

Cop Two steps off the front porch, has his hand around the butt of his weapon, his other hand outstretched as if to hold her back. She stops when she notices Cop One move into the yard, knows she's in real trouble from the way he advances on her. Cop One stands behind her as Cop Two finishes his statement on the investigation.

Joe watches from his yard. Knows they don't believe her.

Dee Dee sees him standing there and bolts in his direction, screaming, "I seen you drag him in there you son-of-a-bitch! You hacked him up in that shed. You kilt my dog, too." Spins back to Cop One. "He done said so. Said he was gonna do me, too!" Swings back to Joe, "That white trash spick stole my dog and you helped her!"

Cop One grabs her arm and threatens to throw her ass in jail if she doesn't shut up. Her mouth pops open as if he'd sprouted two heads. Yanks her arm away and stomps back into the house. Slams the door.

Cop One returns to finish his report.

"Anything I can do about that?" Joe asks.

"Close to harassment. Not there yet. She got family?" the cop asks.

"Don't think so." Joe turns to Pop standing by the front door watching the commotion, yells, "Pop, she got family?"

Pop sees Joe talking to him, turns up his hearing aid and holds his hand to his ear, "What?"

"She got anyone? Family?"

"Naw. Never said she had anyone. Doesn't say much. I stay clear of that one."

Cop One briefly glances up and nods with a slight smile. Keeps writing.

"If she becomes violent, assaults you or your father, give us a call. These things tend to escalate. She may need professional help, but at the moment, she's not a threat. Just a lot of mouth. Here's my card. Case number is at the top. Any more problems, give the dispatcher the case number. We'll come right out."

"Not worried for myself, but my father's eighty-years-old and been in and out of the hospital. Worry for him," Joe says.

"Understand, Mr. Salas. Have a nice day. You folks make it through the storm okay?"

"Fine. Been through worse. Don't build houses like this anymore." Joe shakes the cop's hand and goes back into the house, watches them from the window crawl into their patrol cars and leave.

Pop's standing in the room with his hands on his hips when Joe turns from the window.

"What's going on?"

"Crazy bitch," Joe says walking past him.

"What was all that goings on about you draggin' someone to the shed?" Pop asks following.

"The woman's lost it, Pop. How would I know what's goin' on in her head?"

white trash drama

JOE RIDES HIS bike through waterlogged streets, backed up from overloaded storm drains. Some places he carries his bike through yards to avoid standing pools. Not too much crap lying in the streets, though, just some roofing shingles, palm fronds, camphor tree branches, a pair of shoes, no socks. No skeletonized buildings or collapsed daycare facilities.

Betty's place appears pretty much the same, except the front door's ajar. Car's gone. Joe leans the bike against the porch and goes to the door, stops and listens. Knocks softly. Not sure why it makes a difference if it's loud or not, either way he gets no answer. Knocks harder and calls out, "Betty, you home?" No answer. "Ricky, you guys home?" As if Ricky will invite him in for barbecue and beer.

Joe chances the living room. Sunlight streams through the dirty windows, the rotted boards casting a crucifix shadow on the wall. Dust floats in the sunbeams. Furniture shadows lurk against the walls like waiting predators. The turntable on the record player revolves, the needle hissing at the end of an old Patsy Cline forty-five. His charcoal drawing of Jamie lies shredded on the rug in front of the sofa.

Joe smells puke, sees a bare foot on the floor just inside the hallway. Betty's foot. She's splayed on her stomach, unconscious, badly beaten. He senses she's been here a long time. Knows Ricky's responsible.

"Betty, can you hear me?" Joe kneels and checks her pulse. She's alive. Barely. He searches for the phone, finds it shattered on the floor further down the hall. From the impact on the drywall, it was hurled. Hard.

Betty moans and tries to lift her head.

"It's alright Betty, callin' for help. Where's the other phone?" He asks himself the question, knows she's in no shape to hunt for it.

"I'm sorry," she moans.

"Sorry? Nothing to be sorry for, Betty. Don't talk. Help'll be on the way." As he starts to get up, Betty reaches up and weakly grabs his hand.

"No ..."

"Sorry about what, Betty?" Joe leans down, sees she'd puked blood sometime while lying here.

She tries to squeeze his hand. "I lied," she says, then her eyes close and he wonders if she's unconscious.

"Lied about what?" He rubs her head then starts searching for the phone again.

"Listen!" she cries out, "I need to tell you ..."

"Tell me what?" He waits, but she passes out again.

Scared, he jumps up and moves through the house almost frantic for the second phone, finds it in the middle of her bed on top of bloody sheets. Blood splatters the headboard in a fine crescent spray. Droplets pepper the nightstand and the label of a half empty bottle of tequila.

He dials 911 and gives the operator the address, says someone's hurt and hangs up. Ignores the request to stay on the line until help arrives.

Betty's crying when he returns, urges, under his breath, for the ambulance to move faster as if that could speed it up.

He brushes the hair from her face. "Helps coming, Betty girl. You hang in there."

She quits crying. And quits talking. Sirens howl in the distance. He wants to stand outside to guide them in, but doesn't want to leave her. He sits on the floor in the hallway, back against the wall, holding her hand, rubbing the edge of her fingernail with his thumb. Notices some of her nails are ripped off. Three to the quick. A gash in her scalp is peeled back far enough so Joe can see skull. Her mouth's swollen. New injuries on top of old ones. The right eye's swollen to a slit. Body's nearly all black and blue. Not the first time he's seen her like this, but certainly the worst.

Over the years they were married, Ricky beat the shit out of her on more than a few occasions. And bragged about it. This time more brutally he thought than even Ricky was capable of.

"EMS," Paramedic calls out from the front door, carrying a bright orange bag, stethoscope around his neck, his female partner behind him on the portable radio, calling in.

"Here. Back here!" Joe yells back.

Male paramedic hurries into the house and moves into the tight hallway, sets the bag down, pulls things out.

Joe stands farther down the hall to give him space. He feels useless, wants to hand them stuff.

The female paramedic pulls the gurney close, loaded with equipment on top of the crisp white sheet. Betty's shoved full of IV's and monitors, placed in a neck brace and loaded on the gurney. Joe knows this time it's bad.

Cops are standing in the front yard when Joe comes out.

Female paramedic speaks briefly to one of them then crawls in the back of the ambulance with Betty. The male drives. Two younger cops climb into their cars and leave. Not enough blood and gore here to keep their attention on a hot August afternoon.

"You found her?" Old fat cop asks Joe, scratching the back of his head. His uniform pants hang sag-assed because they sling low on his hips to accommodate the huge gut, shirt so tight Joe can see the cop's furry gut peeking between stressed buttons. Duty leather is dull and worn in places. Cop's gray hair is in desperate need of a barber and in disarray as if he's just gotten out of bed. Like he just doesn't give a shit anymore.

"Yes, sir." Joe answers watching the ambulance turn the corner.

"Who's she to you?" Cop takes a deep breath as if standing in the miserable suffocating humidity is the last place he wants to be. Sweat rolls down the side of his face and it makes Joe's eyes water watching it.

"Been friends since high school," Joe tells him, feels his own sweat break out at his receding hairline.

Cop drops the pad to his side and takes a forced breath. Pulls at collar of his uniform shirt. "Miserable heat," cop says walking to his patrol car. "Sick of it." Opens the passenger door, motions for Joe to get in. Joe reluctantly crawls inside.

Cop squeezes behind the wheel and turns the air on high. Flips all the vents to his side.

Joe sits a little anxious. Wants to get to the hospital.

"Now," the cop says, flipping through pages of his notebook. "Just friends you say? You have a fight, it get out of control, what?"

Joe's stunned the cop's got a whole scenario in his head without ever knowing the facts. Pisses Joe off a little. "Yes. No. No. And I wouldn't know, wasn't there."

Cop turns mildly hostile. "What the hell's that mean?"

"Answered your four questions."

"Smart ass. I hate smart asses. You a smart ass, Joe?"

"No, sir."

Cop looks out the windshield. "You saying you didn't do it, just came up on it?" Looks back at Joe.

"Yes, sir. Found her in the hall like that." Thinks about dropping Ricky's name, but keeps it to himself.

"In the hall? Haven't been in there yet. The hall you say." Cop writes it down.

"Can I go? I need to get to the hospital." Joe's hand clutches the door latch ready to pull it open, knows this case is going to close before the night's over and no one will really care what happened, or why.

"Not done with my fantastic interview yet, Joe. This is the highlight of my day. I live for the days I can wallow in the heat writing information about the ups and downs of white trash and their daily dramas. You part of that drama, Joe? You with your little fag bags chained to your ass with God knows what in 'em. Fingers cut off your gloves. Why does a person cut the fingers off his gloves, Joe?"

"They're biking gloves."

"Are they? You a Harley guy there, Joe? Ride a hog around town, hit the bars, hit women? That why you wear gloves on a hot miserable fucking day like this? They keep your hands neat while you beat the shit out of 'em?"

"No, sir. I have a bicycle. Up there on the porch."

"Bicycle! That one up there? You beat the woman in there, Joe? She finally piss you off 'till you had enough and let her have it? She nag and nag until the thought of smashing your fist into her suck hole seem too good not to?"

"No, sir. Found her that way."

"How about you peel them gloves off there, Joe. Let's see how bruised and red your knuckles are. What do you say?"

Joe peels off the gloves and shoves his hands in the cop's face.

Cop nods, writes stuff on the pad, enough stuff to fill a half page. Joe thinks the cop's putting words in his mouth and writing them on the pad, knows it's gonna end up in a report somewhere with his name attached.

"I can sympathize with you, Joe," Cop sighs. "My wife, she can push and push until I start dreaming about takin' my nine here and emptying the whole mag in her face. That the way you felt, Joe? 'Cause if you did, I can totally relate. Longer you're with 'em, the more you wish they'd just die. Not a day goes by I don't wish I'd come home and she'd be gone. Pack up her shit and not come back." Cop turns to Joe, "I bet that's the way you felt too, but the bitch just wouldn't leave, would she?"

Joe doesn't answer.

"This is damn disappointing, Joe. I'd hoped to wrap this whole thing up tonight, but you're gonna be an asshole about it and not talk. I'm gonna pass it on to our investigators. They'll see right through you, Joe."

"We finished?"

"If you write your information here," Cop says.

Joe takes the pad and pen from the cop's hand and writes down his address and phone number. Hands it back. "Now we're both happy. Any more questions, call me, and I'll keep this white trash thing to minimum. How's that sound, Officer …" Joe reads the cops name tag, "Petri. What do you say?"

"You are a smartass, Joe. Detectives will be contacting you sometime real soon. Now get the hell out of my car."

Joe hurries to his bike and pedals home for the Buick as fast as he can.

POP CREEPS OUT to the back yard wary of anything that moves within the chain link enclosure. Keeps his walkin' stick in his hand, doesn't dare leave the house without it. Memories of the dog attack replay in vivid detail and he wishes it was vague like so many of his memories these days. The attack's so fresh he can still smell the dog's fetid breath—and his own blood that became part of the brew.

The daylily bed's taken a beating, the leaves a green mush mixed with faint colors of what used to be blossoms, eroded from the ground as their tuberous roots suffer in the sun. Shredded leaves of the gardenias litter the yard. Couple of branches split off the Drake Elm and lie in the Ligustrums.

"Plenty to do for outside work," Pop says out loud as if the plants listen. He moves stiffly, still a little tired, so he putters around the back inspecting, just picking leaves and gathering small branches for the trash. Pokes the shrubs with his walkin' stick to flush out snakes seeking drier ground.

The shed's got a new lock. Doesn't remember Joe saying he'd put on a new lock. Wonders what's wrong with the old one and how come he doesn't get a key. Pop shakes it as if it might magically open. Needs his by-pass clippers.

He inspects the outside of the shed for damage and finds fabric snagged by the rose bush. Pulls it off despite thorns still anchored to the cloth like fish hooks. Pop takes his handful of branches, the cloth, and goes to the trash can. Spots a plastic rectangle engraved with letters by the can and pokes it with his walkin' stick. He bends down grunting, picks up a name plate with a bent pin enclosure on the back. The letters, KEYS-LPN. Pop stares at it for a long time.

He looks past the gate to the pond where vultures circle above the dead pine, some as high as a thousand feet in the air, so small he can hardly make out they're birds. Others circle closer now, in a strange ancestral dance, forming a spiral

124

staircase to the heavens, drifting closer and closer. Some alight on branches of the dead pine only to launch off again, and circle with the others higher up.

Pop opens the trash can, finds the black garbage bag, sets the walkin' stick against the house, and removes the twist tie. Pulls out a muddy lab coat and holds it up to the sunlight. Two small holes above the left breast pocket, right where the pin used to be. He pulls out a pair of matching pants, a sock, a tee shirt, a wallet with Keys' driver's license and hospital ID.

He looks back at the dead pine. Seven or eight vultures land on the tree hissing and arguing position. Three drift to the ground.

18

chiggers

IN PURSUIT OF the car keys, Joe blows through the front door like a hurricane gust. He scans the coffee table, the TV tray by Pop's recliner, then scrambles for the kitchen. There Pop is, crouched at the table, a glass of ice tea sweating in front of him untouched.

"The keys?" he asks Pop, breathing hard, forgets the old man doesn't drive anymore.

Pop stares at his glass, wants to broach the *question,* but his tongue's dry and dead. He shakes his head, eyes big and set deep in their sockets, squeezing Keys' name tag in his palm like a dirty little secret.

"Pop! Where's the keys to the damn car?" Joe stands over him yelling at the top of Pop's head, angry he has to waste time asking.

"Don't know. Don't drive, remember?"

"Doesn't mean you haven't seen 'em. You got eyes. You can see things, can't you?" Joe bitches.

"Yeah, I see things. See lots of things. Think I don't notice, but I do. Not just some used up old fool waitin' to die."

"What?" Joe yells, "I just need the damn car keys!"

"I see that. I seen the birds, too."

"What birds?"

"On the dead pine. Lots of activity earlier. Why you suppose that is?"

Joe stands by the window breathing heavy, staring out at the pond trying to think of the last place he had the keys, not listening to most of what Pop's saying.

"Needed my clippers, but you changed the lock on the shed there," Pop says. "Why's that? That mean I'm not allowed in my own shed?"

Joe's thoughts replay the whole night. Suddenly remembers where he's left the keys, ignores Pop frozen at the table with a mouthful of questions, accusations, and the name tag. He bolts for the bathroom, pulls dirty pants from the hamper, and fishes through the pockets. Finds the car keys at the bottom. Doesn't bother to tell Pop where he's going or say good-by. Slams the door leaving Pop to his fears.

BETTY'S CRITICAL WHEN Joe arrives at the local emergency room. Head nurse pulls him from the observation window and barrages him with questions about Betty's insurance and next of kin. Doesn't have either one, he tells her. That's the short and sweet of it. Nurse seems deflated and gives Joe a look as if he's lied to her. She glides back to the nurse's desk and starts on paperwork.

Joe watches Betty on the monitors, the bleep, bleep, spike, flat line, spike, flat line, bleep. Semi-irregular breaths. Tubes everywhere. Hates this place. Same place his Mom died two floors up. Smell's different down here from what he remembers. More antiseptic. Figures folks don't stay in here long enough to lie in piss. Wonders why Betty's still here and not in a room on another floor. Before he finishes the thought, an overworked resident stands next to him, yawns through the back of a hand with an ink pen between his fingers.

"Are you a family member?" he asks, pulling the chart from the door.

"Close as she has. She gonna die?" Joe asks watching the monitor for any change, as if the machine has the sole power whether she lives or dies— as if it's alive and it might've had a bad day so far and take it out on her.

"She may need surgery. We're monitoring the bleeding. If it doesn't stop, we'll operate," resident says. Marks the chart and places it back on the door.

"When will she go? To surgery I mean."

"Can't say yet."

"Can I go in, sit with her?"

"Sure. She's medicated. I don't expect her to come out of it any time soon." Resident turns, yawns again and leaves Joe alone in the hall.

Joe wants to go in but history has him frozen, insists he stay aboard the Disney Land ride of memory hell. He wonders about her words, their urgency, wants to know what she wanted to tell him. He pushes himself into her room, pulls a chair to the bed and sits.

"Betty girl. It was bad this time. Didn't tell the cops anything. Think it drives 'em nuts, too." He doesn't expect her to hear him, but he feels better being able to talk and hold her hand just the same. To his surprise she opens her good eye and focuses on him. Blows a sigh trying to speak.

He sees she's scared. "Hey girl, you're awake. You're in the hospital. Gettin' good care. Just talked to the doctor. He said you're gonna be fine. Just need lots of rest." He hates lying to her, figures she can kick his ass for the story telling when she gets out.

Betty shakes her head and tries to swallow.

Joe moves closer. "Ricky do this?"

She nods and closes her eye.

"He still around you think?"

She nods again. Opens her eye.

"He hang at the same haunts, you think?"

She nods and squeezes his hand.

"We'll find him, Betty girl. He won't get away with it this time." Her hand goes limp. Joe realizes she's passed out on him again. The monitor beeps, beeps, spikes, beeps, beeps, spikes, beeps.

Joe moves from the bed and stands at the window above the parking lot watching people come and go. Wheelchaired mothers cuddling newborns. The sick and injured on the mend, headed home.

Guilt slithers in. Tickles a place deep in his gut where the truths lie, truths he doesn't want to acknowledge because he's weak. Maybe, he thinks, too weak to fight for her. He'd watched Ricky for years carve her life down; hollow out the shell and fill it with whatever toxin he was into at the time. And admits he was too afraid to stop him. The really is, that he is the pussy everyone thinks he is. Sick part is he's been okay with it. Until now.

Joe turns from the window. He'd thought it would be pneumonia or lung cancer to kill her, but the most insidious infection was Ricky. Had been all this time. And he'd allowed him to fester and poison her blood.

Joe kisses Betty on the forehead and leaves the hospital.

SUNSET'S A RICH red-orange against a backdrop of purple washed across the sky. Pop sits at the kitchen table all afternoon. Six or seven times he's drawn to the window and watches the flock of vultures disperse, leaving two or three on the dead pine to preen and digest.

Joe's been gone the entire afternoon and not bothered to call. It's as if he's still a teenager with a curfew. Never been gone this long without calling, though. Pop paces from the back door to the front door, smacking his thigh as he goes. He hasn't felt this unsettled since his war days.

Pulling on the rubber mud boots Mom got him one Christmas; Pop leaves the house with his walkin' stick and limps to the back gate. He stands with a hand on the galvanized railing, heat radiating through the metal from the afternoon sun, doesn't want to let go, but doesn't want to stay. He forces himself to open the gate and move past it, to limp the narrow path through the palmettos and scrub, to watch for water moccasins and coral snakes, to watch for pits in the sand that might knock him off balance and topple him to the ground.

He thinks of what it might be like, trapped back here in the Florida wilds, exposed and defenseless against bobcats and rabid fox. As much as he needs to watch where he walks, he feels the need to reconnoiter the dead pine more.

It takes what seems a long time to limp to the pond, to keep from stumbling; poking the sand ahead of him, looking back for assurance that home is still close by.

And the closer he gets, the more menacing the two remaining vultures.

It's been twenty years since he's been back here, the pines and scrub oaks grown. One blown over at the edge of the pond is still green, roots still half buried in sandy ground like the downed victim of a mugging.

Vultures open their wings as if to take flight, yet remain, watching, like augurs waiting out time.

Exhausted, Pop realizes he must take the exact same steps back to the house. Fears he won't make it. His heart pounds blood through the artery in his neck, his hip aches. Pins and needles sizzle through the bad leg like a shorted connection, and for ten minutes Pop stands on the narrow path, leaning on his stick, breathless. Vultures been comin' around for years, he tells himself. No great conspiracy. Turns to head back to the house when something snaps under his foot.

He jerks his foot off and steps back, sees he's standing on the skeleton of a mid-size dog, tufts of dirty back fur still stuck to the ribs. A crack that runs down to the top of a toothy jaw fissures the skull. The bottom jaw lies two feet from the skull with what could be a leg bone. Chew toys for the opossums and armadillos. He tries convincing himself that's what all the birds were after, but knows in his gut this body's been stripped for weeks. Looks up at the dead pine where the vultures watch, pensive, distrustful.

As dusk descends on the woods, crickets and cicadas start their melodious chanting. Pop turns, spooking three vultures from the edge of the woods line to flap into the trees. Spooks Pop even more.

He can see it in the pine straw. Distorted reddish white lines. He moves closer. A human foot. A body stripped of flesh except for the hands and feet. A head, eyes missing. Fleshy lips and ears stripped away. Black ink covers the remaining flesh stuck to the temple and cheekbone. Flies crawl through the eye sockets to lay eggs in sodden brain matter that the birds can't reach. It's Keys, Pop knows it, remembers watching him in the shadows of the geriatric ward going about the business of killing. Nothing left of the insides. Just a ribcage with a few flesh shreds tethered to bone.

Pop throws his hand to his mouth, limps back to the path and begins to heave. He heaves up lunch and tea and bile. He heaves up responsibility and knows because of him this body lies at the edge of the woods behind his house. He heaves up his lack of empathy for Keys, and heaves up fear someone will find out. He heaves up fear of losing Joe and of being abandoned. He heaves up the fear of dying. And he doesn't remember stumbling through the brush back to the house wielding his walkin' stick, doesn't feel the thorns of the wild blackberry and cat briar slice his hands, and he doesn't see the vultures take flight and circle back to the heavens.

19

happy hour

IT'S A SHIT hole of a place. Cement block construction, no insulation. Used to be, among other things, a sleazy strip joint. Can't fit more than thirty people inside, but the parking lot on a Friday or Saturday night can hold a hundred; more, if they seep into the woods. A few stained, mildewed mattresses lie in the brush, used as flop houses for vagrants when the weather's good, or a quickie from the crack whores that swarm the odor of easy money.

Joe spends the better part of the night trying to run Ricky down, hits all the known hangouts until someone clues him in about this place just over the county line. Just the kind of place Ricky would gravitate to. Lots of easy drugs, easy women, men on the down low, if that's what your bent is. More than enough watered-down liquor. Kind of place Ricky used to take Betty when she was more cooperative. Been more than a few women before, during, and after, and he clearly, from what Joe saw, intended there be more in his immediate future.

Joe finds Betty's Chevy Nova in the parking lot. Feels the cold hood and takes his time easing his way through the crowd. Honky-tonk music blasts through the dark doorway inciting folks to yelling conversation. The Air is thick with cigarette smoke and booze fumes. The window air conditioner's given up trying to cool the place. Congested, it drains stagnant water that turns to a moldy green slime on the bare concrete floor.

Joe spots Ricky in the corner, his arm wrapped around one of the regular bar whores. Joe stands next to him a good five minutes before Ricky pulls his face from the cleavage of the hooker sitting on his lap, his crooked grin melting as Joe's face comes into focus. Recovers nicely, spreads that toxic smirk around like it's free liquor.

"Hey, JoJo. Your old man kick you out, yet?" Ricky laughs in the hooker's breasts. Dribbles beer on the left one and licks it off.

"Talk to you outside?"

"Outside, why the hell would I want to go outside with you, pissant?"

"Betty."

"What about her?" Ricky swallows the last swig of beer, turns and holds the bottle up for the waitress flittering from table to table.

"Outside," Joe says.

Ricky leers up at the hooker, leans back, and shakes his head. "Get up, sweet heart. I'm gonna get rid of this real quick. Keep my spot warm, will ya, darlin'?" Hands her his empty bottle.

Ricky follows Joe outside. Slips something from his pocket into his palm. As they go through the door, he wraps his arm around Joe's shoulders like an old buddy and gives him a hug. They make it as far as the end of the building when he pulls away and shoves Joe into the wall. "What do you want, you little pissant?"

Joe spins in the gravel. "You put her in the hospital."

"Me? Prove it. She probably pissed off one of her other boyfriends."

"She doesn't have a boyfriend."

Ricky bends over resting his hands on his knees, "Except you."

"Been friends since high school. You know that."

"You were a lot more than friends. Or did you think I didn't know?" Ricky savors Joe's expression. "She can't keep her mouth shut. Yeah, didn't think I'd find out, did you?" Ricky straightens up and moves into Joe's face. "She's good when it comes to the secrets there, JoJo. Like the one about her little brat."

"What about him?"

Ricky cocks his head, "You don't know, do you?" Shakes his head and laughs. "She lied to you, too! God, this is too sweet. Man, I got to give it to her. She knows how to screw a guy. Think you got screwed the worse."

"What do you mean?"

"Brat wasn't mine. She said it was yours." Ricky watches Joe's reaction. "Never noticed the resemblance?"

"Liar. She wouldn't keep that from me."

"Spilled it a year after the kid was born." Ricky holds up three fingers then points them at Joe, "Scout's honor."

Joe thinks back, resurrects conversations from distant memory. Little bits and pieces gravitate to the surface. A picture forms. A possible lie. Betty's lie. "That why you messed her up like that?"

"Among other things. Sick of that little bastard's ghost haunting us. Then I find that damn picture you drew. That was the last straw. Know what I mean? Even a pissant like you can understand a man can only be pushed so far." Ricky scoops up a handful of gravel and starts pelting Joe one stone at a time. Like it's a game.

"Then why wouldn't she tell me?" Joe asks trying to deflect the stones with his hands.

"Guess she just didn't want the kid raised by a pussy and turned into a loser like you," Ricky laughs.

Joe lunges. His fist catches Ricky across the brow, knocking him back. Ricky jumps him, *punching, punching, punching* with the brass knuckles he'd slipped from his pocket, then spins and catches Joe under the throat with a choke hold. Joe loses air, his eyes bulge.

"Little fucker," Ricky says breathless, spits the words, "two of you deserve each other. I was glad that sniveling little bastard drowned. No more reminders of you creeping around all the time." Ricky changes positions. Joe's blood soaks through Ricky's shirt sleeve. "Swimming pools are a great thing, JoJo. Real dangerous to little kids, know what I mean? Hear about it all the time."

"No," Joe chokes.

"Yeah, they toddle out when they're not supposed to and right in the water they go." Ricky leans close to Joe's ear, "Especially when someone leaves the sliding doors open so the little bastard can get out. And if you leave his little stuffed bunny in the water, he's sure to go after it. Know what I mean?"

"You drowned him?"

"Arranged it, maybe. Didn't hold him down or nothin'."

"Betty know?"

"Hell no. But even if she did she wouldn't be able to prove it. Really is a perfect murder. I know other ways to commit the perfect murder there, JoJo." Shoves Joe face first in the concrete wall again and punches him in the kidneys hard enough to drop him to his knees.

"You weak pissant. Go home to your daddy, JoJo. Come around me again and I'll kill you, too." Leaves Joe bleeding in the gravel at the back of the building. Returns to his hooker and beer, and never gives another thought to pissant Joe Salas.

"GOD ALMIGHTY, WHAT happened to you?" Pop asks heaving himself from the recliner, clutching the remote.

Joe breezes past him, mumbles "Nothin'," and heads for the bathroom.

"Don't look so much like nothin' to me!" Pop screams after him. Pop's not a screamer. Until now. He crawls out of the recliner knocking the TV tray aside and limps to the bathroom.

"Don't need help. Go back to what you were doin'," Joe says looking in the mirror at the five or six lacerations on his face and head. Some look pretty deep.

"You're as big an idiot as me when you're hurt. Sit down on the crapper there." Pop opens the medicine cabinet and pulls out the Betadine and cotton. Sets them on the edge of the sink and runs hot water. "Haven't seen you like this since you was a freshman in high school when Ricky Vega kicked your ass. Who'd you fight with this time?"

"Same guy," Joe says wincing through Pop's shaky cleaning process. Grabs the wash cloth out of Pop's hand and starts wiping blood. Inspects in the mirror again.

"Thought he's in jail?" Pop opens the Betadine and hands it to Joe.

"Got out. Hand me one of those band aids, will ya?"

"He get out just to kick your ass? What you do to him?" Pop reaches up to touch the particularly nasty cut on Joe's cheek bone.

"Betty."

"Betty? He think something's goin' on?"

"Does it matter? He put her in the hospital, Pop." Joe finishes patching his face, pulls off his bloody shirt, and heads for his bedroom.

"Where you goin'?" Pop calls after him, quick limping down the short hallway.

Back to the hospital," Joe says buttoning a clean shirt. Pushes past the old man and heads for the front door. "Don't wait up. Don't know how long this'll take."

Pop limps to the front window and watches Joe back the Buick out the drive.

HER ROOM IS empty when he arrives. People he passes wince like it hurts them to see his face. Joe steps up to the nurse's desk and asks about Betty's whereabouts.

"Are you family?" nurse asks.

Joe lies, says he's her brother. Only family she has. Figures the lie will work because it's a different nurse.

"In surgery," she says. "Waiting room is on the fourth floor. They have a coffee machine up there."

Joe takes the elevator to surgery and finds the waiting room. He's not alone. Must be five or six different families waiting for news of loved ones. Joe sits in the corner, leans his head back against the wall and closes his eyes. Everything hurts at once. It's the first time he's let himself feel anything in the past two hours.

He opens one eye. A three-year-old little kid holding a toy dinosaur stands by his chair staring up at him. Some kind of red candy goo is smeared around his mouth like lipstick. The kid seems to find Joe particularly fascinating and moves closer. Joe can see the kid wants to touch the ugly bandaged gouges on his face. Kid looks over his shoulder where his mother sits with an infant in a car seat on the floor at her feet, and points to Joe, grunting for her attention.

The mother looks up and notices Joe's damage, signals the kid to her as if what ever happened to Joe will infect her kids. Tries to be polite about it, calls his name, Kevin, or Calvin Something, but the little kid ignores her and the grunting turns to a shrill half-baked whine as if it's too much trouble to scream.

Other people in the room start watching the side show, and now the kid's mother is forced to get up and physically grab him by the arm and drag him back to his seat. She gives Joe a quick smile and admonishes the kid like he can understand a word she says, or cares. Of course, he starts screaming and that starts the infant screaming and she shoots Joe a look as if it's his fault.

Joe moves out into the hallway thinking of what he's gonna say to Betty. What he wants to ask. He can't wrap his brain around Jamie being his kid, doesn't want to, because it's the little things he remembers that crush him. And the *what-might-have-beens.*

With a pneumatic hiss, the double doors open. Surgeon comes through holding his blue scrub hat. Stands at the entrance of the waiting room and asks for the family of Betty Vega. Joe turns and waves.

"She's made it through surgery. We've removed her spleen and her liver was lacerated. A concussion. Three broken ribs and her right radial bone was broken. The orthopedic corrected that."

Surgeon stops talking long enough Joe realizes he's evaluating his beaten face and trying to connect it to the badly beaten woman on his operating table.

"Hurts worse than it looks," Joe says.

"Need to have that checked," surgeon says.

"She gonna make it?"

139

"Next twelve hours will tell." He doesn't smile. Doesn't offer a handshake. "She'll be in recovery for the next hour and then she'll go to ICU. Not much you can do here."

Joe isn't going to argue with that. Suddenly the last three days sit on his shoulders like a lazy elephant. He doesn't remember the drive home. Just shuts down.

20

an elusive reality

PHONE RINGS AROUND seven in the morning. Pop crawls out of bed to answer it. Someone asks for Joe. Pop says he'll go get him, sets the phone down, and wakes Joe from a dead sleep.

Joe gets up hovering halfway between a dream and consciousness, goes to the living room in his underwear and picks up the phone.

"Joe Salas."

Pop stands in the hallway by his bedroom door listening. Turns up his hearing aid. Whoever's on the other end seems to be doing most of the talking because Joe doesn't say much. Joe turns and sits on the sofa, puts his free hand to his head. He pulls the receiver from his ear and it drops in his lap. Doesn't even hang it up. At least Pop doesn't think so. And he doesn't need ears to know whatever was said was bad news. It's written all over Joe's face.

Pop limps to the sofa. "What's wrong there, JoJo?"

Joe rises from his seat and lets out a raging scream, arms extended, hands claw-like. He spins and sweeps the lamp and all the contents off the end table to the floor with one violent sweep. He flips the coffee table and kicks it across the room. Picks up the end table and heaves it into the dining room.

Pop covers his head and scurries back into the hallway. Clutches the doorframe of his bedroom, doesn't realize he's yelling.

Like his plug's been pulled, Joe suddenly stops. Stands in the middle of the room with his chest heaving in and out, shaking. Pop re-enters the room, moving slow as if any quick movement might set Joe off again. He gently pats Joe on the shoulder and guides him to the sofa.

"Son, it's alright there. You calm yourself," he says easing him down.

Joe stares at his bare feet. "Died this morning." Squeezes his eyes shut. "Said she threw a blood clot and never woke up."

Snot rolls down his upper lip racing the tears. "Bastard did it."

Pop sits down next to him, "Who, son?"

"Ricky. He killed her."

"Then the cops will take care of him, JoJo."

Joe shakes his head and rubs his face. "Yeah, he goes back to the joint and five years from now he's out. I don't think so, Pop."

"He'll get more than five, son. Killing's worth life."

"Oh yeah? And what about Jamie?"

"Betty's kid? I'm not following."

"Not just Betty's kid, Pop. Hers and mine." Joe sees the shock in Pop's eyes. "Yeah, mine. Your grandson. She didn't tell me. Learned it yesterday from Ricky."

"That what the fight was about?"

"No, Pop. It's 'cause I'm a worthless piece of shit that can't hold on to anything. Because it's easier to do nothing than fight." Joe lowers his voice. "But you been trying to tell me that for years."

"You can't blame yourself, JoJo. You didn't know."

"Not so simple. He didn't kill just Betty."

Pop tries to remember where Mom kept the brandy. Now would be good time to break it out. Thinks they could both use it. "JoJo, you sit right here. Gonna pour us a drink."

"Don't you want to know who?" Joe asks.

Pop stands up, uses Joe's shoulder for support. "Know what?" Limps towards the kitchen.

"Who else he killed? Aren't you just a little curious?"

"Don't think I want hear it. Where you suppose that brandy is?" He stops suddenly halfway into the dining room. "Didn't drown, did he?"

"Yeah, he drowned. After Ricky lured him out with his bunny. Watched him fall in. Probably watched him struggle and sink to the bottom."

Pop waits through a long pause, thinks that's the end of it. Starts for the kitchen again when Joe continues.

"I wonder if he was standing by the pool when Betty found the boy, or if Ricky just went back in the house and sat in front of the TV drinkin' a beer," Joe says. "Do you think he watched her jump in and drag him to the surface? Heard her panic?" Joe stares at the front door as if it's a movie screen.

Pop stops again, listening.

"I can just picture him in my mind, standing there with a smile while she's on the phone with 911 begging for help, him glad 'cause he finally got rid of the kid. But I don't understand why she never told me."

"I'm grateful your Mom isn't alive," Pop says softly, "to hear this."

Joe glances over, "Me, too. She always wanted grandkids. Had one and didn't even know it. Can you just imagine her with him?"

Pop limps to the kitchen. His pruning shears lie on the countertop as if they mysteriously crawled from the shed. He picks them up and squeezes, lays them back down. Opens the pantry. Way in the back behind the instant potatoes he finds the brandy. He grabs two glasses and takes them back to the living room.

"Whatcha gonna do now?" Pop pours brandy in a glass and hands it to Joe.

"Bury her I guess. She doesn't have anyone else." Joe swallows the whole thing at once. "Don't want her dumped in some unmarked potter's grave," he says wincing from the alcohol. "Wonder if there's space by Jamie? Think she'd like that."

"You gonna call the cops? On Ricky I mean?"

"Nope."

"Whatcha gonna do, then?"

"I'll think of something."

21

sharp tools

ISN'T MUCH STUFF to show for a life, Joe tells himself. Walks through Betty's dark apartment, a manila envelope in his hand filled with Betty's meager personal effects, a box of black garbage bags, and a half eaten happy meal he'd picked up on the way over. He sits on the sofa chewing fries, thinking about where he's gonna find the money to bury Betty, wonders if funeral homes offer payment plans.

He thinks about the day Jamie must have been conceived. Not like it was planned, happened so fast. Surprised him as much as her. Weirded them both out. He never thought much about it after that. Sex felt out of place in the separate lives they'd both made. And it never happened again.

Car door slams. Joe doesn't bother to get up and check. Doesn't care.

Ricky stands at the screen door, his silhouette dark and imposing. Joe knows who it is just by the form, feels the familiar prickling of his skin on the back of his neck from anger, maybe fear.

"What are you doing here, pissant?" Ricky asks pulling the screen door back.

Joe drops his head. Mouth dries up. Heart pounds against his chest.

Ricky moves into the room, the screen door slamming behind him. He stops in front of Joe, grinning, reeks of stale beer and sweat soured too long on the skin, Joe's blood dried on the sleeve of his shirt. Stares down at the top of Joe's bald spot.

"Takin' care of Betty's arrangements," Joe says, cocking his head, mumbles, "thanks to you."

"Thanks to who? What did you say, pissant!" Ricky yells.

Spit peppers the top of Joe's head. "Nothin'. I'll come back later."

"I don't think so. This here's my place now. Get the hell out!" Throws the car keys on the coffee table.

"Not leavin' without her things. She wanted me to take care of her stuff."

Ricky straightens up and considers him coldly. "There's nothin' here, JoJo! She had nothin' but shit," swings around an outstretched hand, "as you can see. Not givin' up the car. And this apartment's mine now."

"Don't want 'em. Just her personal stuff."

Ricky steps back and kicks the coffee table. "Get it and go. Don't want any reminders of her or you." Turns on the heel of his brand-new cowboy boot and heads for the kitchen. "You got five minutes and then I kick your ass again."

Joe pulls a garbage bag from the box and moves around the room picking up photos and knickknacks, collecting and bagging, thinking the whole time about the bedroom and how he doesn't want to go in there. He doesn't want to go in the hallway where gelatinous bloody puke sticks to the fake wood vinyl. He can hear Ricky open the refrigerator, the sound of glass bottles clinking, Ricky's boots thumping across the floor, dominant, aggressive.

"Yeah, you got it all figured out, don't you?" Joe mutters quietly, goes out, sets the full bag by the back of the car and goes back in to start another. He yanks a second bag from the box and flicks it two or three times to open it up. Joe enters the hallway and avoids Ricky's boot imprint where it's stamped in the bloody puke as if he hasn't even seen it. Seems Ricky's way of letting him know how insignificant Betty really was.

Joe opens the closet door to bags of Jamie's baby things, memories Betty valued most. And a paper bag on the top shelf. Joe pulls it down and opens it. Jamie's moldy bunny peers up at him, the torn ear now a reminder of Betty.

"She kept that shit?" Ricky asks stepping up behind him.

Joe jumps. Almost drops the bunny. Closes its bag and drops it in the garbage bag.

"Told her to get rid of it. All of it. Sick of her cryin' over it all the time," Ricky says turning for the bedroom. "Always was weak."

Pulling things off hangers, Joe listens while Ricky goes on and on in the other room about how much of loser Betty was, and how much better his life is going to be without her.

From the edge of the doorway, Joe can see Ricky lying on the bloody bed sheet drinkin' beer. Sees him pick up the bottle of tequila, try to wipe the clotted blood off with the palm of his hand and survey the contents to be sure no one drank any while he was out. Satisfied, he sets it back on the nightstand, leans back, crosses his feet at the ankles and lights a cigarette.

"Why didn't she tell me?" Joe asks, stuffing things in the bag. He knows Ricky can hear him, doesn't expect an answer. And a good five minutes pass before Joe hears the empty beer bottle drop to the floor and Ricky speaks up.

"Now why in the hell would I let her do a stupid thing like that? What would I get out of it? Women. Ever notice how stupid they are?" Ricky waits through a long pause. "You still there, JoJo?"

Joe freezes with the bag in his hand. "Yeah, still here." Cigarette smoke creeps from the bedroom and drifts under his nose.

"Some too stupid to live. I see it this way, JoJo. It's the law of natural selection. She was a weak defect that fucked another weak defect and they in turn bore another weak defect. I've single-handedly eliminated a potential disaster to humankind. They should give me a damn medal for it."

"You threatened her if she told?"

"Not really. Said I'd cut your head off and weight it down with concrete and dump it in the lake where she likes to fish. Said maybe one day she'd be pulling on the line and up would pop your head," Ricky laughs. "Sent my boys around every now and then to let her know it was still possible even with me in the joint. See what I mean there, JoJo? After the kid died, you think she didn't believe I'd do it?"

Joe nods slowly like he agrees with him.

"Then why beat her to death?"

"She needed put in her place. Always did know how to push my buttons. I'd whipped her ass worse than that before. Guess she can't take it like she used to. Anyway, she's out of her misery."

Joe gently sets the bag on the floor, walks into the kitchen, opens the drawer next to the stove and retrieves Betty's large fish filet knife. He walks out of the kitchen, down the hall and into the bedroom where Ricky lies trying to finish the last of the tequila, cigarette burning between his fingers.

Joe doesn't speak. He makes no gestures, just one fluid movement to the bed where he jams the knife into Ricky's sternum, shredding his aorta.

There's little fight from Ricky's end, mostly a gurgling sound Joe can't tell if it comes from blood or tequila. Joe stands over the bed, neither angry nor relieved, watches the panic in Ricky's face and finds it oddly attractive. He takes the cigarette from Ricky's fingers and crushes it in the ashtray on the nightstand. "See, rabid dogs should be put out of their misery, too. Not just *sick ones!!*" Joe yells.

Joe calms and goes to the bathroom and returns with a washcloth for stuffing into the wound in Ricky's chest to stanch the bleeding. He washes the filet knife in the kitchen sink and places it back in the drawer, retrieves the bag from the hallway, goes out to the Buick, and opens the trunk lid.

Back in the house, Joe pulls three or four more bags from the box and goes out and lines the trunk. Returns to pick Ricky up, carry him out to the Buick, and drop him in the trunk.

"See, not so weak," Joe says slamming the lid. Calmly goes back into the house to finish collecting Betty's things.

POP STARES OUT the kitchen window watching the dead pine. Not so much bird activity now, only a few latecomers that drift in, pick the bones, and leave. He thinks about the grandson he never knew, thinks about Keys rotting in the woods. He wonders what happened to his son, where he went wrong. Worries what he can do about it. Wonders if he should do anything at all. Jumps guiltily when the doorbell rings.

At the door, a sharp dressed man. Pop places him as a funeral director, doesn't think they usually come to the house. Pop looks past the guy to the driveway, doesn't see a funeral van. Just a generic, bland Ford. Pop suspects it's a cop. It's confirmed when the guy holds his badge and ID up for inspection.

"Mr. Salas? I'm Detective Croy."

"Which one?"

Detective opens a small leather-bound notebook and quickly reads. "Joseph."

"Not here. This about Betty?" Pop asks waving the detective into the house.

"Yes, sir. Did you know her?"

"Not so well. JoJo and her were friends." Pop props himself against his recliner to relieve the pain in his hip.

"Will he be home soon?"

"Never can tell with him. Think he might be at her place taking care of arrangements. Not sure how he's gonna pay for it all. We don't got a pot to piss in," Pop whines. Thinks how his attitude must sound to the cop. "Been a shitty week. Don't know when to keep my mouth shut," turns towards the kitchen. "Get you somethin' cold? Got Sodas. Water. Guessing you can't have beer."

"No, thank you, Mr. Salas. I'll try to catch up with him there. Have a nice day."

Pop stands alone in the dining room worrying when they'll come for Joe. When they'll come for him for knowin' about it. He limps to the window and watches the Ford back out of the driveway and move down the street. He sees Dee Dee at the mailbox in her robe watching, too. She squints at the house to see who's peeking back. Slams the mailbox shut and waddles back to the house.

WITH RICKY IN the trunk, Joe hasn't got room for much else. He piles baby blankets on top of the body along with the two black bags filled with pictures. Slams the trunk hard. The rest of the bags he piles in the backseat.

In the apartment, he stands at the bedroom door surveying what's in it worth taking, feels an odd sense of calm as if he's watching from outside his own body. Nothing in the past three weeks registers emotion. Not grief or hate. Not forgiveness or revenge. Nothing has smell anymore. Nothing has color. And he's glad. He's been forced to close the door on a family he didn't even know he had. He's been allowed to escape from the possibilities and hide from reality. The way too often his life's been.

A knock on the screen door and Joe leans out, knows by sight, it's the detective the fat cop promised. Yet, not even the threat of discovery with a dead guy in his trunk brings emotion to the surface, and for Joe Salas, it's probably his saving grace.

"Mr. Salas?" Detective Croy asks from behind the screen door. His eyes settle for a moment on the slow heal all over Joe's face. Makes a mental note to ask about it.

"That's me," Joe says, holds the screen open for the detective to come in. Cologne follows. A faint whiff of an ironed shirt. Aftershave. "You here about, Betty?" Joe picks up a bag off the floor and stuffs in the last of the clothing.

"I'm Detective Croy. I'm sorry for your loss. My understanding is you were not related. Just friends?" Detective scans disapprovingly around the room. Like it's too dirty to stand in and he might catch something contagious.

"Since high school," Joe says leaving for the bedroom. Croy follows, notices the bloody puke in the hallway and carefully steps over it.

"What are you doing here, Mr. Salas?"

"Packin' some of her things together. What she wanted me to do."

"I can't let you do that, sir. You're going to need to leave. This is a crime scene now. After the technicians finish, we can release it back to you."

Joe stands with his hand on the closet door. "Didn't know that."

"Come outside with me, Mr. Salas," Croy gestures with is hand. Cuff links on his starched shirt glint in the light.

151

Joe abandons his project with Croy behind him, stops at the back of the Buick.

"You take those things from the house?" Croy asks pulling off his jacket and laying it carefully over his arm. Takes a handkerchief from his trouser pocket and gently blots the sweat on his trimmed brow.

"So far. Just got here. I gotta give 'em back?"

"Everything's evidence. It needs to be processed. You can drop them here."

Joe opens the back door and pulls out three garbage bags of clothes, sets them on the ground at the detective's feet. Notices how polished his shoes are. Spit shined.

"Does she live with anyone?" Croy asks jotting in his notebook.

"No. Lived alone. After her boy died that is."

"How did he die?"

"Drowned. At the house she lived at before. Couldn't stay in it because of what happened. He was only three." Joe moves to the back of the Buick and leans against the trunk, crosses his arms over his chest.

"Sorry to hear that. Did she have a boyfriend?"

"An ex-husband. Just got paroled."

"That would be Ricky Vega?" Croy blots his brow again, gazes longingly towards his car and the cold bottled water now sweating on the console.

"Yeah. Guess you know about him then," Joe nods.

"Were you acquainted with him? See him since his release?"

"Known him since high school. Saw him a week ago right here," Joe says tapping the trunk lid with his forefinger.

Annoyed he has to drag the information out of him, Croy asks, "Well, did she go back to him?"

"Not exactly. Didn't give her a choice. He came back and took up where he left off. I think he started beating on her right off. To keep her in her place, see."

"Why do you say that?" Croy jots more notes.

"The black eye and busted lip was a clue."

Croy gestures to Joe's face. "What happened there?"

"It matter?"

"She's beat. You're beat. It's an honest question."

"I didn't beat her. Didn't kill her, either."

"I didn't say you did. The officer on scene said you didn't have a mark on you when he interviewed you. Those aren't more than a couple of days old. Why didn't she call the police if she was being abused?"

Joe watches sweat bead across Croy's tight forehead and waits for him to blot it dry as if it's a contest on how fast it'll happen.

"Was pointed out to me that she was just another white trash drama. You all know about her history if you know his. She wasn't going to risk getting swept up in his shit again. You people didn't believe her the first time. Why'd she think you'd believe her now?" Joe leans over and spits on the ground. "Took her hits and kept her mouth shut."

Croy blots his forehead, flips the hanky to the dry side. Blots again. "Did Vega have something to do with her death?"

"Oh, I don't know. He beat the shit out of her on a regular basis and she was beaten bad enough to go to the hospital. Then she dies. You'd classify that as a what? An accident? Not that it matters."

"This is a homicide, Mr. Salas."

"And she had to die to get your attention? Or is this just, just, I don't know…you," agitated, Joe holds up fingers to signal quotations, "*investigate*", and then say case closed?"

Croy pulls at his tie. "Becoming hostile won't help the investigation, Mr. Salas."

"Neither will you. We finished now?" Joe pulls the car keys from his pants.

"For now. We'll contact you if we have any more questions. We know where you live."

"Yeah, I betcha do. Let me know when you're done with her place." Joe hands Croy the keys to Betty's apartment.

"Do you know of any place Vega might frequent?" Croy runs the hanky around the inside of his shirt collar.

"Weren't friends. Don't care. Any roach hole, maybe," Joe tells him closing the door of the Buick. Drives off with Ricky in the trunk and Croy baking in the heat.

22

a small slice of...

HE'S CONCERNED HOW the heat in the trunk might affect Ricky's features. Doesn't want it to slough off or stink real bad while he's working on it. Worries about it all the way home.

Joe parks in the driveway trying to decide the best time to take Ricky out of the trunk, suspects the fat bitch will be watching, call the cops and start her crap all over again. He's sick of talking to cops, sick of having to explain what he's doing as if it's anyone's business. Just needs the head anyway. Body's a lot a trouble. Too much dead weight to drag around. Checks his watch, gets out, and opens the trunk. He takes out the two black garbage bags, leans in and sniffs. No smell yet. Closes the trunk and lugs the bags to the front door.

Pop opens the door looking down at the bags, starts to say something.

"Don't wanna talk," Joe says, dragging the bags inside. Sets them by the coffee table and goes to the kitchen.

"I do!" Pop yells after him, glances at the bags again, torn whether to look inside or follow Joe to the kitchen. Bags win.

Pop sits on the sofa and pulls one between his legs, unties the knot and spreads the opening. His chest deflates as if punched in the gut. He gently takes out a photograph of Jamie taken two months before his death, knows instantly who it is.

Wide grin. Eyes full of piss and vinegar. He can see in the picture, all the family that came before this little boy, bits and pieces of those still alive and those long dead. The eyes of his father. Face of his mother. Mom's smile. He's crushed under the grief still warm from the death of his wife.

"I took all the pictures. Everything that she had that was his," Joe says. "Tried to get her stuff, but the cops said I couldn't take it yet. They don't know I got this stuff." Flops in the recliner and takes a swig of cold beer.

Pop nods, swiping a tear from the edge of his eye. He sets the picture on the coffee table and scrutinizes the others one by one. Bag seems empty, but his fingers sense something soft and matted. Gingerly he extracts it, looks at it, puzzled for a moment. A moldy stuffed bunny.

Joe glances at it then looks away. He fights the tears that well up, swallows more from the bottle and stares at the window trying to think of anything that'll keep him from falling apart. He drops the bottle to his lap, clutching it tightly, forces his eyes to the window and shudders into a deep uncontrollable sob.

Helpless, Pop stands up, limps to his room and shuts the door.

HE'S CAREFUL TO watch for the lights in Dee Dee's house. Sees them go off one by one until he's reasonably certain she's asleep and not haunting the windows. Pop doesn't leave his room all evening. Joe takes it as a sign that the time's right and slips out into the backyard, a full moon illuminating in soft grays, deepening the shadows of the underbrush. He unlocks the shed, grabs the tarp, and lays it out by the gate. He pulls Ricky from the trunk, covers him with the tarp, opens the gate, and drags the body to the foot of the dead pine.

Joe stands for some time thinking about the last few days, takes satisfaction in his actions, and wonders if this is what the beginning of addiction feels like. Flips back the tarp from Ricky's head, drops to his knees, and with finger tips and moonlight, closely examines the cooled face.

"Betcha never thought you'd end up like this, did you?" Joe whispers tracing the bone structure of Ricky's face. Pinches the neck. "Want to be famous?" Joe glances over at Keys' remains. "He wants to be famous, too. Hey Keys, brought you a buddy. He was an asshole, too. You two just get acquainted. I gotta get stuff from the shed."

Joe enjoys the moonlight walk back to the shed, pleased he doesn't even need a flashlight. He pulls the machete from the wall and slips a garbage bag from the box. Feels the edge of the blade and flips on the light. He opens a drawer on the bench and takes out a whet stone. Slides the blade over the stone until the edge cuts into his forefinger. Puts his bloody finger to his lips and smiles.

Spinning on his heel, he whacks the bench. The blade digs into the wood, vibrating in his hand. He wedges out the gleaming steel, turns off the light, and heads back to the pond.

Whizzy bugs trill in the dense underbrush, and beyond the pond is the mournful cry of some unidentifiable creature.

Joe pulls the tarp from the body and throws it behind him. Strips off Ricky's cowboy shirt, wife beater T-shirt, belt. Pulls off the tight new cowboy boots. Rolls off the socks, then the jeans. He's not surprised to see Ricky doesn't wear underwear.

Not such a big guy with him stretched out like this, Joe thinks, standing over the body. Mouth just made him seem bigger. He rolls Ricky face down, stretches the neck from the shoulders, and squats down on his knees.

After two practice swings that stop just short of contact, Joe raises the blade and with one whack severs Ricky's head. It flips over on the right side of the face. Joe grabs the severed head by the hair and pulls it from the body. Lets it bleed out at the waterline.

He's not sure how long it takes for a head to bleed out, decides to rifle through Ricky's pants while he waits. The wallet retrieved from the pocket of Ricky's jeans gives up thirty-six hundred dollars. Forty-five cents in the front pocket. A guilty pleasure. Okay, not so guilty.

"Where did you get this kind of cash, asshole?" Holds the bills close to his face and counts them again. "God only knows. Whores or drugs," Joe mumbles, standing up. Throws the wallet on the tarp and pockets the cash. "Use your money to bury Betty. There's an irony in there somewhere."

Cool air blows off the pond, the moonlight reflecting on the water. "Only fair." Pushes the head around with the toe of his shoe. He sweeps the garbage bag off the ground, drops in the severed head, and parks it on the tarp while he drags Ricky's body by the feet next to Keys. Gives it a limp farewell kick.

With the clothing wrapped in the tarp under his arm, and the severed head slung over his shoulder, Joe enjoys the moonlit walk home.

DEE DEE PULLS the sleeping mask from her face and struggles with the sheet. Her little feet hit the floor and hurry to the bathroom. Hand over her mouth, desperate to make it on time, she doesn't bother to turn on the light, just throws herself in front of the toilet and shoves her face through the seat. She pukes and heaves in wintergreen-steeped water until shaking and exhausted. And it isn't the first time. She realizes the frequency of the attacks, suspects the gall bladder, a self-diagnosis from the Internet. Not puking blood, so concludes it's probably not an ulcer.

She rolls over and sits on the cold tile, wipes her mouth with the back of her hand. Rubs her gut to decide if it's safe to get up yet.

Great loneliness fills her insides like a ruptured dam, and at thirty-seven she's hugging the toilet like it's her best friend. Thinks she might be dying, but she's too afraid to see a doctor. Not exactly. More like defiant. She doesn't want to hear the bla, bla, bla about her weight, her high blood pressure, her fat intake, her pebble shits, just so they can threaten her with a heart attack or stroke. Possible infertility. She thinks about infertility and it makes her cry.

With great effort she stands up and flips on the light to examine her face in the mirror, reviews the list of symptoms of gall bladder disease. Seem to be more zits. That was one symptom. Throws a leg on the toilet seat and rubs her thick thigh hunting for newly spun spider veins. Read varicose veins were a symptom, too, wonders how big a spider vein got before it was classified as varicose. Then there were the hemorrhoids. They were on the list. Not going there. Doesn't think she has any.

Chinese say gall disorders are linked to anger. That's what she read, pulls her underwear down and sits on the toilet. Pulls off a couple spins of toilet paper and wipes her eyes.

JOE CLOSES THE shed door and flips on the light. Plunks the severed head on the workbench and pulls a sheet of rice paper from the roll. Removes Ricky's head from the bag, but it still bleeds. Not a lot, but enough to make the bag messy. He takes a roll of Duct Tape and wraps it around and around the neck, crisscrossing several times until the opening is sealed. Good old Duct Tape. A million and one uses.

Joe washes the head in the sink, dries it with paper towels and holds the chin in his hand with moist fingers to manipulate the jaw, "Hey, pissant, look at me. No body," Joe says. He pulls the head close to his face. "Who's the size of a pissant, now?"

It's much easier managing the head without the body, Joe thinks. He can work on the bench with plenty of light and take his time; be a little more creative with his paint mediums. Wants to try some of the metallic colors new on the market. He's found a beautiful blue green metallic paint that he thinks would bring in a tropical feel to the work, a change from the standard black ink in Gyotaku.

Joe paints the skin with delicate precision. Not too much paint, not too thin. Determines the best profile is the left. Nothing wrong with the right, but the left is free of scars and anomalies.

Joe pins the bottom of the rice paper under the jaw, takes his time rolling the paper across the chin, the cheek, eye socket. Attaches a pin in the hairline and gently presses the nose. Barely touches the brow. Doesn't want the eyebrow to absorb too much paint or it'll come out goopy with no hair definition.

All in all, it takes about an hour to produce the print he wants. He hangs it on the pegboard where the metallic paint catches the light and shimmers against the white paper background. Not as much definition in the eye as Keys, but Joe thinks he can paint it in later. He washes Ricky's face again to remove all the green paint and repeats the process with a different color. Copper is nice. By the time he finishes, Joe's used four different colors. He overlays two of the prints for a multidimensional work. Likes them all. Seeing them lined up on the pegboard, he realizes at some point he's got to mat and frame them.

He regrets not severing Keys' head for more printing opportunities, but hey, it's a learning process. Can't keep Ricky's head indefinitely, wonders how well it will keep in the freezer. Head's too big for a gallon sized Ziploc freezer bag, though. Wonders if one of those food vacuum sealers will work. Thinks he remembers one tucked away in the pantry.

23

a tight fit

HAUNTING THE HOUSE in her bare feet, Dee Dee moves from room to room as if there's nothing to do. She denies the condition of her home, the condition of herself, the depression she's spiraling into. She's almost finished her old bottle of Xanax. Doesn't think she can sleep or function without it.

Holding the new bottle, the thought of taking larger doses visits her more often now. One pill, two pills, three. Six pills, seven, an even dozen.

She stands at the kitchen sink annoyed there are no clean dishes or drinking glasses, looks out the window where fog threads through the back yard, and the moon appears as if it's sitting on the fence by the Salas's shed, illuminating the door. But it's not the moon that's backlighting the shed. The light is on.

AFTER COLLECTING THE Food Saver machine and a roll of the large size bags, Joe roots through the refrigerator for leftovers. Hasn't eaten since before he killed Ricky and he's famished.

A hunk of roast beef with a few potatoes sits on a plate covered by plastic wrap. Can't be more than a few days old. He doesn't remember eating it whenever. Realizes Pop's cooked again. Can't blame the old guy. He hasn't been home much to supervise him, either. Grateful, Joe pulls the wrapping off the plate, and despite the lack of silverware, stands at the sink to eat. He sets the empty plate in the sink, goes back to the fridge, and retrieves a bottle of beer. Takes it and the Food Saver to the shed, and closes the door.

Joe pops the cap off the beer and swallows a third of it. Ricky's head stares out with slackened mouth, tongue pushed against the side of the cheek, the tip protruding between the teeth. Joe plugs in the Food Saver, notices how Ricky's eyes seem fixed on the door as if waiting for company to start the party.

Duct Tape seems to be holding.

Joe takes the roll of Food Saver bags and holds it next to the severed head. Looks like it'll fit. He measures by eye and cuts a section off the roll with scissors. Takes one end of the cut section, sticks it in the Food Saver, locks it in place. Presses the button and the machine purrs to life. Light goes out so Joe opens the lid, removes the bag and checks the end seal.

"What do you think?" Joe takes the bag and struggles to stretch the open end over Ricky's head. It's a tight fit. Like trying to squeeze a sticky bowling ball into one leg of a pair of pantyhose. Makes Ricky look like a cartoon armed robber— face disfigured and wrinkled, nose pushed to one side. Joe wonders if this is how Ricky looked when he was jumping bank counters and shoving a gun in the faces of terrified tellers, poor Betty sitting in the car humming along with the radio while he was making, what she thought, was a deposit. She said she didn't know Ricky was making a forced withdrawal. Cops didn't buy it, couldn't imagine anyone that stupid.

"Feel familiar? You deserved to be arrested for criminal ugliness. Probably like it. Gives you comfort. Well, get used to it, you're gonna be in it awhile," Joe says. He lays the head in front of the Food Saver and shuts the lid on the open seam. Clamps the lid and presses the button. Motor strains and strains. At first the plastic bag begins to cling nicely around the face, but can't hold the seal and puffs back open.

Another failure. Bag's too small and they just don't come any bigger. He grabs his beer and sits on the bench next to the severed head crammed in the Food Saver bag. Must be something else he can use.

Joe checks his watch. Sun will be up in an hour or so. He finishes the beer and walks back to the house.

Pop's in the kitchen making coffee. He gives Joe a faded smile, plugs in the pot, looks out the window. "Foggy out there."

"What are you doin' up so early? Not even sunup yet."

"Slept enough. Whatcha doin' up?"

"Couldn't sleep. Thought I'd take some of Betty's things and store them in the shed there. Plenty of room," Joe lies. Sort of. He's gonna store her stuff in there, but he's got bigger priorities. Doesn't think Pop needs to know what.

"You take out the things you want to keep in the house?"

Pop sits at the table in his underwear waiting for the coffee to finish. "Some on the table out there. Pictures mostly. Maybe clear a spot on the book shelves for 'em. Cute little guy." It's all Pop wants to say.

Joe doesn't pursue it, doesn't want conversation now while Ricky's head heats up and starts to rot on the bench. Needs to freeze it as soon as possible.

"You got stuff for a breakfast?"

"Yeah, got my bran flakes."

"Any prunes?"

"Plenty of prunes. Want me to stab a few in a bowl for you?"

"I'll pass. Got a lot to do. Know where that bag storage sealer thing is?" Joe asks rummaging through the pantry.

"Food Saver?" Pop asks watching.

"Naw, the other thing. That thing we got Mom one Christmas. You know, where you plug in the vacuum cleaner there and it sucks all the air out? For blankets and that."

Joe's mildly aggravated Pop's not catching on. Bends at the waist and gestures as if it will explain it better. "The things that squish the air out and make 'em real small so you can store things in half the space?"

Pop draws a blank. Peers up at Joe like a dog caught crapping the floor. "Don't know, JoJo. Might check the hall closet."

Exasperated, Joe throws his hands up.

DEE DEE STANDS at the sliding glass door for a good half hour sipping Pepto-Bismol from the bottle, trying to talk herself into unlocking the door. An argument rages in her head. One side insists she see what Joe's up to, the other rebuts to keep her nose out of it. A statement, *"It'll just cause trouble,"* bobs to the surface like a channel marker. Then she thinks about the dog, sees the bowl of rotted food, and rage boils beneath the skin. Her face flushes at the thought of her dog slaughtered in that shed, of how her neighbor has made a mockery of her life.

She slams the Pepto-Bismol on the counter and throws open the lock.

The moon, setting in the distance, cuts through an onyx sky. Dee Dee creeps through the back yard and peers between the slats in the fence. The shed door is slightly ajar. She thinks she might find evidence of the dog, perhaps the collar and tags, maybe something else incriminating. Drugs. A Meth lab. Heard on the news there were lots of white people operating meth labs in old neighborhoods like this, buying all the cold meds off the shelves and setting up little family kitchen pharmaceutical companies. She could sneak into the shed, take a look see and be out before Joe knew she'd been there.

There's enough light to pick her way through the two yards to the shed. She watches the Salas's back door as she creeps across the yard, rehearses under her breath what to say if caught. Nothing she comes up with makes any sense. Might say she's sleepwalking, but doesn't think he'll buy it.

Weird croaking and the harsh note clucking of a coot calls from the pond as she moves through the fog, raising the hair on the back of her neck.

POP POURS COFFEE, bends over, and inhales the aroma. Takes the cup and a small bowl to the table, and pours in bran flakes. Twists the loose lid off the prunes and starts to sit.

Forgot his paper. Turns for the door, realizes he's in his underwear. It's mostly still dark. Decides he can make it to the driveway and back before anyone sees him. He takes the walkin' stick propped by the back door and slips into the early morning dew.

LAMP LIGHT REFLECTS the fog around the shed door, a pulsing mist that moves and shifts with the slightest disruption. Dee Dee's hand pulls on the handle ever so slowly to muffle any squeak or groan that might escape the hinges. It pivots

166

silently. A moth flutters in the doorway, smacks her forehead and escapes into the mist. She bites her lip to suppress the squeal.

Another moth assaults the lantern burning on the bench and bare bulb hanging from the ceiling, slamming into them time and time again until fine particles of dust disperse in the still air, the moth circling the room for a way out.

Dee Dee tiptoes in, swatting the moth, surveys the room, the boxes along the wall, the garden tools posted on the pegboard, the art materials. She sees the plastic bag next to the Food Saver. Moves closer. Not sure what it is. She stretches to touch it, tilts her head. Leans over to inspect exactly what it is she's looking at. The moment she feels the plastic, she slaps her hand to her mouth and stumbles backward toward the door, fighting the eruption of a scream pushing through her fingers.

Pop scuttles across the foggy driveway with the newspaper in one hand, walkin' stick in the other, ready to beat the shit out of anything that might come at him in the dark. Feels cool air circulate the bottom of his droopy drawers, his boys swaying free in the breeze. Opens the gate and steps through.

Like a ghost out of the mist, Dee Dee's in a dead run from the shed, the scream replaced with a deep throated gurgling. Pop sees her coming at him and isn't sure what to do. Lifts his walkin' stick in the air just in case. About the time she hits the gate, he can tell she doesn't even notice him standing there. Blows past him and disappears in the dark.

"God, Almighty," he says. Hears her sliding glass door slam shut. Thinks he can hear her scream. Could be mistaken.

Joe steps out the back door with the Hoover Mighty Mite and a box of vacuum storage bags from the hall closet.

"You see that?" Pop asks looking back at the gate.

Joe stops, "See what?"

"Dee Dee. Come from the shed, I think. Flew past me like her ass is on fire."

"Shit."

"What's that? Whatcha suppose she's doing back here in the damn dark?"

"Like I said before, Pop, woman's nuts."

"Yeah, but now she's creepin' 'round the yard. Think she's dangerous?"

"Who knows. Don't worry about it, Pop. Eat your breakfast."

"Gonna get a shower, clean up some after I eat. Fix you somethin'?"

"Ate already. I gotta go back to work." Joe fades in the fog, leaves Pop to his paper and prunes.

Joe drops the Mighty Mite and storage bags on the floor of the shed. Starts to sweat despite the coolness of the air. He knows she's seen Ricky, thinks of what to do about it. Probably on the phone right now with the cops.

Gotta get rid of Ricky. He opens the freezer.

THE STRING OF heavy breathing, guttural groans, and stifled screams that come into 911, at first, sounds more like a pervert masturbating to a phone sex site than someone wanting to report a homicide. At least that's what the dispatcher thinks. It wouldn't be the first time. And not until the words, 'severed head in the shed' does the dispatcher check her CAD screen to see what units are available to take the call. Waves to the supervisor to pick up on the other line. Not gonna handle this one alone.

The scream that Dee Dee's manages to control finally makes its way to the outside world, and what's recorded on the 911 line forces the dispatcher to yank the headset off and sling it to the console. Dee Dee's voice can still be heard through its ear piece by the next call-taker over. Now everyone in communications is awake.

It takes fifteen minutes to dissect Dee Dee's complaint, instructions to calm down, pick through the rambling hysteria of her earlier complaints. Dispatcher types in Dee Dee's address and up pops the previous calls to the residence, all concluded with *"unfounded."* Sub-note to report: Complainant signal twenty. Loosely translated means she's nuts. Policy demands a unit respond nonetheless, and one begrudgingly responds ten minutes before the end of shift.

Dee Dee swallows two Xanax at the kitchen sink and sucks water straight from the faucet. She trembles uncontrollably. Briefly considers she may be going insane. Might be the pills.

24

handcuffed frozen chicken

"GOD, YOU BETTER get some sleep." Pop looks down at the top of Joe's shiny bald spot ringed in gray hair, wondering when he turned old. Turns back to the kitchen counter, "Don't like what's goin' on much, either. Not one bit with that one." Pours a coffee and surveys the pond through the window.

"That who?" Soon as the question departs his lips, Joe regrets asking. His mind speeds along trying to think of something to distract Pop from answering. Bad timing to bring all up now.

"Never mind. Medical examiner finished up with Betty and I gotta go to the funeral home about her arrangements. Funeral guy said cremation's cheaper. Cuts the cost over half the burying rate."

"Paying it with what? Can't suck blood from a turnip." Pop leans in, "Someone's already got a hold of you, though. Need more than just clean clothes there. Need sleep. Betty's goin' nowhere."

Pushing himself from the table, Joe sets his coffee mug in the sink. "Just need to get it taken care of. You can understand that can't you?" It's a rhetorical question. And even if he wanted to, Pop has no time to answer because of the doorbell.

Pop limps out to catch the door. Joe stands at the kitchen window watching the skies above the dead pine. Sun blisters through the haze.

"Cops back again, JoJo!" Pop yells from the front window, "got *three* cars out at Dee Dee's place this time."

"Been expectin' 'em," Joe mutters to the window.

Cop One's huge frame towers under the low ceiling of the living room. Pop's got him in a conversation about some article in the paper. Something about a phone scam and old people, or maybe it's about old people committing a phone scam, Joe's not sure which. Cop seems relieved Joe's come in to change the subject.

"Mr. Salas, sorry to bother you folks again so early."

"What's the problem this time, Officer?"

"Your neighbor."

"God, not again," Joe says. Sits on the arm of the sofa.

Pop pipes up, "Crazy bitch. Creeps around the back yard in the dark!"

Joe grits his teeth, "Pop, I'll handle this."

"I know. Go clean the kitchen." Pop limps out.

"She was in your yard last night?"

"Before daybreak. Pop seen her when he was goin' for the paper."

"Would that be somewhere around the shed out back?"

"Yeah. Think Pop said she came from over there. Didn't say anything to him, though."

"Okay," cop sighs, "I need to check the shed again, Mr. Salas." Reaches for his mic and calls a number. Transmission comes back. A series of numbers. Joe's clueless what it all means.

"After you," Cop says motioning for Joe to lead him through the house.

Pop grabs his walkin' stick and falls in line behind. Doesn't want to miss anything.

Dee Dee waits at the Salas's gate sentineled by three uniformed cops when Joe comes out, like she's in command and waited years to serve the subpoena.

Joe leads them to the shed and opens the door.

"It's right there," Dee Dee orders. Flails her arm and stumbles backward. One of the cops grabs her elbow to keep her from falling over.

Joe flips on the light and stands aside.

Cop One steps in, turns back to Dee Dee. She's waiting excitedly, eyes wide, wringing her shirt tail in her hands, a grin stretched across her face. Shakes her head as if mandating him to go on.

Cop pulls his Maglite from his belt and sweeps it around the dark corners of the shed, watching Dee Dee from the corner of his eye.

She impatiently moves closer, inches from the doorway, barely able to control the anticipation. "The bench. It was right on the bench there!" she says shaking her finger.

Cop takes the Maglite and examines the bench. Pokes through the art stuff, clear plastic boxes stacked against the wall. No sign of a traumatic crime scene.

"You said, right here?" Cop taps the Maglite on the bench where Ricky's head was.

"Are you deaf?" She yells. "See the blood?"

"I see paint. Red paint. But it's paint. Not blood."

Dee Dee moves closer, stretches her neck for a better view. "Oh, hell no it's not paint. It's a man's head in a plastic bag. Right there!" she insists.

Cop opens the freezer, shines the light inside. Stops abruptly. Slowly turns back to the others, his face drawn and serious. Tilts his head at the cop closest to Dee Dee like it's some unspoken instruction. Doesn't go unnoticed by Dee Dee.

"What? What's in there? It's there, isn't it? Told you he kilt him." Twists back to Joe standing against the fence behind her chewing a thumbnail. "You didn't think they wouldn't find it, did you?"

Cop reaches in and pulls something wrapped in plastic from the freezer.

Dee Dee clutches her chest, sways, and screams. Cops around her stiffen.

Cop plunks it on the bench. "Rump roast. About the right size," he says.

"Sirloin tip actually," Joe corrects.

"Oh, hell no. I did *not* see a damned roast. It was a man's head in a plastic bag. I saw his eyes, his mouth!" Turns to Joe. "You're gonna to pay for this, you hear me!!" she screams. Balls up her fist and lunges at him.

Cop grabs her arm and twists it behind her back. She kicks at Joe, flipping one of her mules off, sending it through the doorway. "You mother *fucker!* I'll take you out, you hear me!!" she shrieks again.

Joe tries not to smile, tries not to make it seem like he's enjoying it so much. Throws his hands up and walks towards the house. He hears commotion in the shed like they've thrown her to the ground and have a good fight on their hands.

Pop limps behind and pokes Joe in the ass with his walkin' stick. "You do that?"

"Do what, Pop? Told you she was nuts. Thinks I murdered a rump roast," Joe says walking through the gate to the front yard. Sits on the front steps to wait for the cops.

Pop huffs up to the door. Stops. Starts to say something but lets it drop and goes inside.

Dee Dee's escorted in handcuffs to one of the patrol cars lining the cul-de-sac. She stumbles and steps out of her pink mules, kicking them ahead. Cop following behind sweeps them up, slings them into the car.

Joe watches her get pinned against the fender and searched. Thinks that can't be pleasant for either side.

She yells obscenities as a hand slides under her arms, down her side, between her legs. She threatens a lawsuit, threatens to call the NAACP, threatens an ass whipping if they'd just take off the cuffs. She's shoved into the backseat and kicks a mule off the floorboard into the street with a stubbly foot. Cop throws it back in and slams the door.

Joe can see her rocking back and forth in the backseat shrieking at the back of the cops' head. Feels bad for the guy as they drive off, knows she's gonna be like that all the way to wherever it is they're going. Joe wants to wave, but concedes that would be pushing it.

Cop One locks up Dee Dee's house and walks back to Joe.

"What's gonna happen to her?"

Cop drops the key in an envelope, "Baker acted. She'll be on a seventy-two hour hold for evaluation and they'll determine what to do with her." Writes her name across the fold. "Needs something." Wipes his forehead on his shirt sleeve.

Joe stands up, "Wanna come in and write that up? Get you somethin' cold."

Cop nods. Follows Joe inside and sits at the kitchen table to finish the report. Pop shuffles in from the bathroom, glances from Joe to the cop and back again.

"Get a drink for the officer here, Pop," Joe says. "Cold drink in the fridge there."

"Just put 'em in. Don't know they're cold yet," Pop mutters. Takes a glass from the drain board, opens the fridge

174

and takes out a Mr. Pibb. Can is still warm. Opens the freezer. Ricky's head stares from its plastic shroud. Pop slams the freezer shut.

"Outa ice," Pop gasps leaning against the fridge. "Got ice in the freezer out back. I'll go get it."

"Tap water's fine," Cop says without looking up. Starts on the narrative.

Pop nods slowly, fills a glass from the tap and sets it on the table. Turns back to the sink gripping the cool porcelain with a death grip hoping the cop doesn't notice the horror on his face. "Gotta take a *shit*," he says limping out of the room.

Cop's head pops up like he's not sure what he just heard.

"Like I said, says whatever," Joe shrugs.

A shadow momentarily blocks the sunlight from the kitchen window. Joe turns to investigate. Sun is hot and brilliant. Window goes dark again. Joe stretches, sees the black tip of a wing by the roof.

Vultures. There's maybe ten of them scattered between the pond and his yard, three roosted on the chain link fence like they know who feeds them and wanting more. Four or five swarm the house.

Joe's arm hair rises in quills. He shuts the blind and pours a cup of coffee but can't drink it.

"I'll swing by Life Stream and issue her a trespass warning tonight when I come back on duty. If she comes on your property again, she goes to jail. Sign here, I'll be on my way, Mr. Salas."

"Life stream?"

"Mental health facility." Cop pushes the report across the table, gathers the rest of his papers and tucks them into his aluminum report holder.

Joe makes an *S* with a long string attached on the signature line and pushes the report back across the table. Follows the cop to the front door.

"Hope this gives you folks a little peace," cop says stepping onto the walkway. A shadow passes over his head. A vulture banks right and flaps its wings to gain altitude over the roofline. A second drifts from the roofline in the opposite direction and floats around to the side of the house.

Pop pushes past Joe and steps out onto the porch with his walkin' stick just as a vulture lands, out of steam, in the big oak by the driveway.

"I've never seen them come this close to people," cop says. Steps farther down the sidewalk to see where they're going.

"There's whole shit load of 'em," Pop says to distract him. "They migrate."

"They migrate?"

"They migrate from all over. What the paper says."

Cop holds the report holder over his brow to block the sun and count the birds. "What, they decided this county was the place to vacation this year?"

"Always been here. More now I suppose," Pop says, "loosin' their habitat. Damn developers. Gotta go somewhere."

"Yeah, well glad I don't live with them. You folks have a good day."

The instant the cop's out of sight, Pop hustles to the backyard, drivin' his walkin' stick deep in the ground in a step, stab, step, stab, step, stab. Opens the gate and stops.

There must be two dozen, maybe more now clustered around the yard. Most around the shed. Some strain the thin top branches of the drake elm tree. Others clumsily try to roost on the ligustrum shrubs. A tight black column spirals from the dead pine to the sky like a tornado funnel.

Pop thinks every vulture in the country has heard about this place and decided to come see for themselves. Could be hundreds.

Pop slowly backs away from the gate and closes it. Hurries back to the front. Doesn't waste any time getting to the kitchen, wonders where Joe's disappeared to. Stands at the refrigerator wanting to open the freezer, yet terrified to. Could have been mistaken, what he saw, might have been his eyes playing tricks on him, just like Dee Dee's. The moment he places a hand on the freezer, Joe enters the kitchen with a folder and his keys.

Pop searches Joe's face for something to confirm his fears. Joe sets the folder on the table, removes a document and reads. Shoves it back in.

"Gotta go, Pop. Be back before dinner."

"What about the freezer?"

"What about it?"

"You gonna leave it in there?"

"Leave what?"

Pop opens the freezer. A roasting chicken sits between the ice trays and the box of ice cream sandwiches.

"I'll start the chicken when I get back. Take it out to thaw, will ya?"

Pop nods. Sort of. Stands chilled in front of the open freezer as Joe leaves the kitchen and well after he hears the Buick back out of the drive.

25

bubble wrapped silence

ON THE FRONT seat of the Buick is a small box wrapped in brown paper, a label stuck to the folded flaps on top. Betty's ashes. Money gleaned from Ricky's pants gave him enough money to cremate her, but not enough for a plot to put her in. Funeral guy said lots of people keep their loved ones at home. In jars. So, Joe drives around town thinking and ends up at the art store at the Triangle Center next to the Bingo parlor and Fat Man's Pool Hall.

Navigating narrow aisles, Joe picks up framing mats in different colors, eight twenty-four by thirty-six frames, and five packages of gold leaf. Lady behind the register recognizes him from the gallery, asks why she hasn't seen him lately.

Joe tells her his father's been sick and leaves it at that, wonders if she knows the story and is testing him, or if she's been left out of the loop. Joe pockets the change and as he heads for the door, notices a stack of flyers on the counter.

"These free?"

"Take all you want," she says. "Gentleman came in and dropped those off. Exciting, isn't it? Chance to have your work looked at by a big-time art critic? Are you going to enter?"

"Maybe. See if I can whip somethin' up. Thanks."

Back in the car, Joe picks up the box. "Gonna give it another try, Betty girl. Gonna do it for both of us." Sets the box back on the passenger seat and drops the transmission into reverse. "For all three of us."

Joe parks the Buick in the Gator's Restaurant parking lot and stands at the entrance of the boardwalk. He scans for the regulars, folks who fish from the railing rain or shine.

A small group is clustered under one of the gazebos, fishing equipment spread across the benches and concrete walkway. Joe remembers meeting them from time to time when he'd come looking for Betty, good people who just wanted to be left alone, each with a story no one seemed to want to hear. She understood that, was one of them, too.

He didn't think it would be this hard. Didn't think memories cut with such sharp edges, even slicing to the bone the moment he saw their sad faces.

Recognition of him reminded them of her, reminded them she was gone for good. Beyond the eye contact, no one spoke for lack of words that might bring comfort. They all knew it wouldn't. Not really. He appreciated the silence, couldn't bare the condolences even if they were offered. Not from them. The guilt of failing Betty kept a tight grip and for a while, at least, he felt he deserved it, needed the self-inflicted soul lashing until it bled.

"Anyone catching crappies today?" he asks avoiding the contents of the buckets. Remembers Betty's warning about looking into a fisherman's bucket, some rule about it being rude or against the law, something like that. He didn't understand it. But for her sake, he keeps his nose out of the buckets.

A little black woman turns from the railing, "Got me five."

"Can I buy 'em?"

"How ya gonna get 'em home?"

Joe hadn't thought through the logistics. Needed them alive if possible.

"I'll buy the bucket, too. Twenty cover it?"

She sets her pole against the railing, picks up the bucket, and holds it out. "Nice ones," she assures him wiping her cheek with the back of her hand.

Joe takes the bucket handle, but she doesn't release it. Places her free hand on his and says, "Her favorites," and turns loose.

Joe hands her the twenty and carves out a weak smile. Carries on a whole conversation with her in his head in the few seconds they hold eye contact. Suddenly realizes they're all watching him.

Joe starts for the car then stops. Looks down at the bucket of small fish. "She cared for you all. After Jamie, you gave her what little peace she ever had. Just wanted you to know that." Joe continues to the car and never looks back.

POP STANDS AT the back gate as a strong wind blows off the pond into the yard rustling the river birches. For a long time, he stares out, talking to himself, talking to Mom. Maybe praying.

His hand's been wrapped around the gate so long, feeling is gone in the fingertips, but he doesn't notice. He feels déjà vu, feels pulled to the pond, but doesn't move. He knows what's down there, thinks he knows, struggles with a conflict raging between truth and denial.

A lone vulture drifts on the thermals high above him, sweeping in larger and larger circles, a scout searching for today's meal. Pop knows it means nothing's left at the pond other than bone, knows if he goes down looking for the body he might find it. Headless. That would confirm it. In his mind. But at a cost. He clings to the denial, even though tattered and transparent, shoves the truth to the darkest corners of his mind, locked up so it never sees the light of day. Never speak of it again. He turns from the gate and goes inside. Shuts the door.

JOE SETS THE bucket of fish on the bench after adding a little fresh water from the hose. He doesn't want them sucking all the air out and turning into smelly floaters before he starts the project.

He puts Betty's box on the bench next to the fish and inventories his purchases. Lays the frames on the floor and the mats below each. Unpins one of the head prints and sweeps it from one frame to the other, knows custom color matching is critical.

After forty-five minutes of comparison, he's made his selection and begins layering prints onto the frames. Cuts the excess paper from the print where the pin holes are stained with blood. He cleans the glass on both sides with window cleaner and paper towels, adds the mat, the print, the backing. Glues waxed brown paper to the back of the frame. Installs the hangers.

With the finished piece on the bench, Joe stands back. For the first time in his pathetic life he feels the rush of accomplishment, the pride of good work. He knows it's good, knows when shown it will be unlike anything ever submitted. Feels it in his bones.

Two hours later, five framed prints are lined along the top of the bench. Joe chews his thumb nail and smiles. He carefully wraps each print in bubble wrap and slides them into a heavy-duty cardboard box. Seals the top with packing tape and places the box by the door.

He checks his watch. Should have been back in the house hours ago. Remembers telling Pop to thaw the chicken. Pours more fresh water to the bucket of crappies, grabs Betty's box, and locks the shed.

Kitchen's dark when he comes in. Joe flips on the light and notices the kitchen is just as he left it. The roasting chicken sits thawed in the sink. He goes into the living room where a small light burns by Pop's chair. An empty can of Ravioli sits on the tray next to the recliner with a fork in it. He knows the old man didn't even bother to heat it up.

Pop's bedroom door's shut. Joe senses the loneliness, flops on the sofa with Betty's box in his lap. Scans the photographs of Jamie that surround him, stuck on every flat surface in the room. The old cuckoo clock ticks endlessly on the wall.

26

miami vice

CRAPPIES COME OUT better than Joe anticipates. He creates a nice print—four of them in a school happily swimming along on crisp white rice paper. The iridescent blues and greens give movement for the eye, stimulate the imagination. He packs this print separately, a teaser for the really good stuff. Wraps the dead fish themselves in aluminum foil and a plastic bag, and chunks them into the trash along with any blood evidence of Keys or Ricky Vega. Cleans up, moves his art material to one side so Pop can have free reign of the shed again.

Stepping out of the shed, he hears Dee Dee's sliding glass door close and peers through the slats. Sees she's back. Figures her seventy-two-hour sentence is up and she must not have been nuts enough to be forced into staying longer. He hadn't thought she would. Doesn't matter so much now. Nothing left for her to get into.

POP'S IN HIS recliner, the remote in his hand moving in a slow circular motion. Whatever's on the TV screen has got his full attention. Joe stands next to his chair several seconds before clearing his throat. Pop briefly glances up, slides back into the program after pointing to the screen.

"JoJo."

"Whatcha watchin', Pop?"

"One of these cop shows."

"Law and Order?" Joe sits on the arm of the sofa, watches the screen through the commercials.

"Not so much. C.S.I. stuff. Amazing what cops can piece together with a little bit of a person. D. N. A. Don't ask what it stands for, though. Long name, so they just call it D.N.A."

"I know what DNA is, Pop. Glad you found somethin' to watch. Cleared out the shed for you. The key is on the nail by the back door." Joe stands up.

Pop continues to watch the screen, waves the remote at the TV again. "Had this one fella who cops think killed his girlfriend. Couldn't prove it. Found a body. Or what was left of it. Skull was bashed into a million pieces so cops couldn't prove who it was or how it died."

"They can get it from bone marrow and teeth," Joe says as if an authority.

"Nope. Burned up. Burnin' did something to the marrow. Never found the teeth. So many bone fragments missing, they couldn't figure it out. Stupid to leave it where someone might find it, though. Guess he didn't think that far ahead."

"He go to jail?"

"Free as a bird. Got a new girlfriend now, too." Pop turns slightly. "Now if it was me, I'd a buried what was left in different places so even if it got dug up, say, sometime in the future, no one would recognize it as bones, don't ya see.

184

They'd just bulldoze over it and go right on. That's what I'd do," he pauses, "if it was me."

A weird silence creeps in. Joe notices Betty's box has been placed on a small table, Jamie's little bunny propped against it, surrounded by photos of Jamie, Betty, and a few photos of Pop, Mom, and himself. Not unlike the shrine at Betty's place, but without the candles.

"Thought I'd put 'em together. That okay there with you?" Pop says to the TV.

Joe wonders how Pop knows he's looking at it without looking up. "Okay, I suppose. She should be with Jamie and not on a table, though. Doesn't seem right."

"Might be right. But you can only do what you can do."

Joe stares at the TV. "Gonna drop off some stuff at the new gallery. Thought maybe you'd like to ride along and we'd grab some lunch at the diner."

Pop clicks off the TV, and grabs his walkin' stick. "I'll get my shoes."

POP WATCHES IN the side mirror as Joe opens the trunk and takes out the boxes of artwork. From the passenger seat, he can see inside the gallery and the flurry of activity as workmen install portable walls and lighting, dodge around boxes and crates of artwork from all over the state. It's all mysterious to him. Doesn't know what's in the boxes Joe's carrying through the door, doesn't know why the boy can't get a real job.

Old resentments weasel their way into his chest, try to settle in. But he knows this is Joe's dream and he hasn't had much to look forward to lately. Lost an awful lot. He senses a change in Joe even though Joe acts the same.

A city patrol car eases by and Pop worries. Worries if Joe's smart enough to take care of the details.

As if watching a muted TV, Pop sees Joe ask one of the workmen a question. Joe nods, and then approaches a trim middle-aged woman who appears to be supervising, clipboard in hand, reading glasses perched on the end of her nose. Pop wonders if she's the one who canned him. Sees them shake hands. Probably not. But then, Pop thinks, Joe has a way of covering his real feelings. Could be doing it now.

Joe slides his boxes against the wall, takes the time to fill out paperwork and hand it back. Smiles while he does it. Something else Pop hasn't seen in a while. Notices Joe's stride is a bit livelier when he bounds down the steps back to the car.

His curiosity gets the best of him. "What's going on?"

"Entering stuff in a contest. Big art critic gonna pick out the best ones and they go on tour. The work gets written up in magazines and newspapers."

"The drawings you used to do?"

"Not so much drawings anymore."

Pop wants to know exactly what. Fears a reaction if he asks. Clutches the denial even harder. "Tour. That like music folks?" Pop's confused.

"Sort of. Giving a big grand prize."

"How grand?"

"Couple a grand, I think. Ready to eat?" Joe asks pulling out onto the street.

"Ready when you are."

"SHE THE ONE?" Pop, asks concerned, squeezing ketchup on his fries.

"Who?"

"The woman you used to work for. In the art place there." Peels the top of the bun from the burger and coats it with ketchup.

186

"The Botox Queen? Hardly. Want the pickle?" Joe asks holding the pickle by one end.

Pop points at a spot next to the burger with a French fry. "Right here."

"It's a different gallery, Pop. Didn't you notice?"

Pop shrugs. Swallows. Doesn't remember if it was the same place or not. Wasn't the kind of place he'd brag about to his V.F.W. buddies.

"Botox Queen. Why do you call her that?"

"They inject Botox in the lines in your face to fix wrinkles. Freezes your face so you can't smile right. She used a lot of it."

"What ever happened to her? She still around?"

"Couldn't tell you. Don't keep up with her. It matter?"

The question catches Pop in the middle of a bite that causes him to pause a second while his mind wraps around how he's going to answer it without sounding obvious. "Not so much. Got an extra napkin there?"

Joe separates a napkin from the stack by his plate and hands it over. "Dee Dee's back."

"Think she's better?"

"Better than what?"

"Not creepin' around our mess, stickin' her nose where it doesn't belong. Think she'll mind her own business?"

"How would I know, Pop?" Joe stuffs the last of his burger in his mouth and chews hard as if to eat Pop's question.

"Just sayin' gotta watch that one. All I'm sayin'. When will you hear from 'em?"

"From who?" Joe separates a ten and two ones from bills wadded in what the fat cop had called the little fag bags on his belt. Looks up at Pop. "From who?"

"How will you know if you got picked?"

"They'll call. Why?"

"Nothin'. Just wondering."

187

"MS. SADIE, HOW chew wan these unpacked?" Julio asks in his soft Cuban accent, one delicate hand on his slim hip, the other flipped up, his pen targeting the stack of boxes against the wall.

"The workmen, they finish, but I no thin the lighting right yet." Overtly turns his head to gaze at the shirtless twenty-year old stretched on the ladder adjusting the track lighting. "I thin maybe we keep a few of then lonker," he grins.

"In a word. Hell no. Not paying overtime for your social life, Julio. Think I'm blind? Another half hour, you'll be licking him off the ladder."

"Thas two words," Julio corrects. He spins around to look up at the worker again, runs his fingers slowly through his thick blond hair showing lots of teeth. "Chew know, tha is no a bad idea. Why I no thin of tha?"

Sadie looks at a package, pulls a razor knife from her jacket pocket and flicks the blade forward with her thumb. "Like you haven't."

Julio turns back, notices the razor knife in her hand. "Ooo, Ms. Sadie the *sadist.*" Stretches his lips as he says the word sadist. "Tha wha chew are, chew know?" Somewhat deflated, he swooshes past her to the first stack of boxes. "Where we start?"

Sadie steps up to the first box, swipes her red hair behind her ear, and hands Julio the clipboard and a roll of sticky labels. "Write the information that's on the box on a label and I'll unpack." Razor slits taped seams, the flaps pop up. She pulls out an oil painting of an old farmhouse surrounded by rolling fields. "God, I hope it gets better than this," she mumbles.

"I heard chew."

"I don't care. Are you writing this down?" she asks tapping the box flap with the razor.

"I'm writing, I'm writing. So pushy."

Two hours into it and most of the boxes are unpacked. A surreally varied collection of artworks litters the hardwood floor, name labels tagged on their backs. Some of the work's pretty good, but most runs to the plain, expected, unimpressive. Nothing exciting enough to cause a stir in their stagnating art circles.

"There's four or five more," Sadie says checking her watch. "Finish these and we'll come back tonight and figure out who goes where. Lamont flies in tonight. I have two hours to change and get to the airport. Hear he doesn't like to be kept waiting." Sadie retracts the blade and slaps it in Julio's open hand like a surgical instrument. "Lighting boy's leaving, too," she smiles quickly.

"Chew *are* a sadist. Cruel too," Julio whines. Pouts in lighting boy's direction. "Chew leavin me in this dark morgue alone? They no do that in Miami!" he calls after her. "I could get accosted here all by myself."

"Dream on!" she yells back before the door slams.

ALONE IN THE dim light of the building, it is a little creepy. Julio opens a box, pulls out a drawing. A nude. Well, half nude. Female. Depressing. He can't stand the silence and flips on the boom box left by the workmen. Tunes to a Latin station and salsas back to the boxes, doesn't care people waiting for the green light can see him through the open floor-to-ceiling windows.

Two boxes sit tucked into a dark corner. Julio would have missed them if he hadn't needed space to put empty boxes. Scoots the bigger box out with his foot and shoves it closer to an overhead pot light. Opens the smaller one and unwinds the bubble wrap. Iridescent colors glitter under the light. The fish seem to be fighting against an invisible tide.

27

cake mix

DAYS ARE GETTING shorter. Leaves of the wild grape, stretched through the scrub oaks along the woods, yellowing. Brown seed pods on the crepe myrtles drying out. Pop notices it all.

"Cooler weather soon," he says opening the door of the Buick and noticing Dee Dee's front door shut. Mutters, "Nosey bitch."

"What?" Joe asks.

Pop leans on his walkin' stick for support in the driveway, "Nothin'."

"What are you gonna do tonight? Any good movies showing?" Joe asks. Strokes his ulterior motive like a cat.

"A good one," Pop says shuffling to the front door. Turns and grins. "*Soylent Green.*"

Joe rolls his eyes and unlocks the front door. "You've seen that, what, twenty times?"

"Who the hell cares? It's a classic. No real men like Heston around anymore. Think they're running the *Omega*

Man after that. Gonna try and stay up for that one. Don't know, though."

Walks through the door and sets the walkin' stick next to the recliner, "We can make some popcorn. Make an evening of it. What do you say?" he asks hopeful.

Joe stops. "Got stuff to do right now. Probably make the second feature. That good for you?"

"Sounds like a date." Pop grins, flopping into the recliner.

"Well, if it's a date, that's sad for both of us," Joe says walking through the kitchen.

"Yeah well, gotta get 'em where you can," Pop laughs to himself.

JOE GOES TO the shed and retrieves the shovel and the eight-pound maul. No trash bag. Peers through the fence to see if Dee Dee's snooping around. Nothing stares back but the creepy garden gnome. He takes the tools, closes the shed, and walks through the brush to the dead pine.

Shadows stretch long across palmettos pushing through sugar sand, the woods hushed as if waiting to see what victim he's brought this time. He stands over the remains of Keys and headless Ricky. Pokes what remains of the Dee Dee dog with his shoe. Not so much left. Varmints have dragged off most of it.

He stands a long time just contemplating. Decides he needs something flat. And hard. He meanders around the pond and up the slope, finds several concrete blocks left over from the old neighborhood construction site decades ago. Carries them back to where the bones wait and places them side by side.

He picks up Keys' skeleton. It breaks apart in his hand. Skull drops, rolls, stops at Ricky's foot.

191

Joe lays the bones on the rocks, swings the maul over his shoulder and pulverizes the femur bone with one deep penetrating thump.

It takes a good forty-five minutes to bash 'em all. He scoops up the dog bones and smashes them with the rest. The last three or four blows fracture the blocks, now a cake mix of cement and bone fragments that embed in his socks and shoe strings.

Joe's T-shirt bleeds sweat at the neck and armpits, his arms and upper shoulders ache with fatigue. He leans on the shovel to catch his breath, head shaking to a silent statement about helicopters.

"Sorry boys. Too big to leave lying around where cops might see 'em from the air. You can thank old Pop for that. Who knew?" He picks through the remains for teeth, broken and whole, and tucks them into his pocket. Scrapes the bone fragments and cement crumbles together in a neat pile.

He digs fifteen three-foot-deep holes in a quarter mile radius around the pond. Some at the water's edge, others deep in the woods and fills each hole with a half shovelful of pulverized concrete and bone. Tops them off with dirt and rotted leaves mixed up like compost. Briefly considers burning it, but decides not to. Smoke might cause someone to report it. Pictures a guy with a friendly Smoky the Bear hat and a badge asking, 'Whatcha burning back here, boy?'

'Oh, nothin' much. Just body parts.'

Can't risk it.

It's dark when he finishes up. Collects pine straw and leaves—sprinkles them over the area where the bodies were. "Never would know what was down here," Joe says. Claps his hands together and shrugs a bit of ache out of his shoulders.

With the shovel in one hand and the maul in the other, Joe trudges back to the shed. Big moon, sky clear of clouds and vultures.

192

28

stretched perspective

THE FRAGRANCE OF incense perfumes the darkened hallway, slips benignly into the crevices of aging brick and crumbling mortar as Sadie and the art critic enter, their high-tempo footsteps echoing.

Julio appears from a doorway, a bit gray and nervous. Despite his anticipation of the famed art critic, Lamont Fisher, meeting him face to face fails as an occasion for his cheerful welcome.

Sadie, clearly worn from waiting through the two-hour flight delay and annoyed at the lack of studio light, notices Julio's demeanor, takes it as a sign something's wrong. "Mr. Fisher, this is my assistant, Julio," moves past him to the main gallery, "what did we finally end up with?"

Julio drops in behind her, realizes he's rudely cut in front of Lamont. Abruptly stops and squeezes against the wall to let Lamont move ahead. "I tag and place by category as chew can see …"

"What happened to the lights?" Sadie finds the switch, flips it up and down. Turns to Julio, "What happen to the lights?"

Hands raised in surrender, Julio says, "I no nothin Ms. Sadie. They just no come on. Just a few of those little lights work, chew know? None of the big ones." He stands amid oil, pastel, acrylic, artwork—near a cluster of sculptures in the middle of the floor.

"It been very scary staying here alone. I toll chew we need that lighting guy to stay a little lonker, but chew say, 'No, no,' and send him away." Flaps his hands. "Now we have no light."

Sadie shoots him a look and turns to Lamont standing in his raincoat, hands clasped in front as if waiting for a bus. As a half-assed apology, she says, "Sorry. It's the little things, you know?"

Lamont raises a hand as if to dismiss her, the work littering the walls interesting him more than her problems. Picks up two small oil paintings and tilts them into the light.

Julio takes the chance to speak to Sadie without Lamont overhearing.

"Ms. Sadie, I thin chew shoo see this." Pulls at her coat sleeve toward the dark corner.

"I can't right now." Whispers, "I need to get Lamont to his hotel. Bad turbulence."

Julio, eyes shining, "Are chew comin back? If no, I leave, too?"

Seems too excited about leaving. Sadie doesn't think she'll be coming back tonight. By the time she gets Lamont settled in, the night'll be pretty much shot. And Lamont's bored.

It's taken her eight months to get him here, negotiations of terms, housing—the best bed and breakfast in the county—all expenses paid, including airfare. The press releases are sent, the invitations out for the gallery opening, the caterers contacted, and every other frigging detail.

"Then be here at five sharp," she tells him. "And the incense …" she announces as he begins to fade down the hall, "It's nice. We'll use it." Sadie heads for the door, realizes Lamont has disappeared. What if he's wandering lost in the halls or gotten locked in one of the empty rooms upstairs? Doors tend to stick in these old buildings.

"Have you seen …?"

Julio isn't listening, but watching Lamont bent over a row of frames. She can't see what it is, knows it has Lamont's attention. Which means it better have hers, too.

Lamont carries one of the framed pieces to the nearest pathetic light. He hands it off to Sadie and retrieves another, holds it, too, to the light and nods. "Who's this?"

Sadie checks the back for the artist information. "Never heard of him. He lives right here in the city, though. I'm surprised I don't know him."

"An unknown. Really? What fun," Lamont says, inspecting the newly installed gallery walls. "We'll get that lighting issue taken care of, won't we?"

Julio, arm bent at the elbow, chin on top of his hand, raises an eyebrow at Sadie. "I toll her, Mr. Fisher, she shoo no let the workmen go yet, but what do I know." Turns his nose up and pouts.

"Let's get you settled in, Mr. Fisher, and we'll hit this first thing tomorrow," Sadie says shooting Julio a glare.

"Chew need me to call the workmen tonight, Ms. Sadie?"

Grits her teeth, "Yes, why don't you do that."

Julio hurries down the hallway yelling, "Chew two have a very good night. I have one, too!"

195

EVEN SHE CAN'T take the mess anymore. And three days in a mental ward have given Dee Dee a little perspective, even though she's not a hundred percent convinced that what she saw wasn't the real deal.

Okay, so she has a slight drug problem. She drops the dog's bowl, crusted food and all, in a garbage bag along with the torn muu muu and empty snack food boxes. Still hurts thinking about him. Misses his greeting at the front door, misses the way he hogs the bed in the afternoon, misses the way he begged to share the Cheez-its.

Makes her think of asshole Joe Salas. That's what she calls him now. Asshole Joe Salas who killed her dog. The shrink Doc tried to convince her it was the drugs. Maybe they caused her to hallucinate it all, and as for the dog, maybe it ran off and got a better offer. Shrink even suggested it found a girlfriend. Dogs do that, he'd said.

She told him she had the dogs nuts sliced off, so a girlfriend wasn't likely. That's how they left it. Session over. Her free seventy-two-hour mental fix and a new prescription for Serentil.

Three hours later and the house is clean, laundry going, fresh sheets on the bed. Dee Dee settles in the recliner after a hot shower, starts working on her ragged nails with a file and keeps one eye on the Salas's driveway.

A STEP, PAUSE, step, pause. Lydia glances through her mascara gloom, compelled by rumor and the sizzle of small town excitement that draws her out like a rat in the dark, and a chance to meet the famous art critic, Lamont Fisher. A catch for sure, despite the familiar grinding of sour grapes.

She likes Sadie well enough. No, she really doesn't. She resents her for hooking this critic in a gallery less than six-months old with its fresh paint and distressed walls. And she knows anyone who's anyone is sure to be on the invite list. But not her. Well, that's not stopping her from dropping by a few days before the big ceremony on a secret mission—to procure one of those invites or at least see what the competition is. If any.

Julio spots her scurrying behind an unfinished wall pretending to inspect the spackling. The fur alarm on the back of his neck goes off. Hand in the air, he makes a bee line to Sadie's location somewhere in the building between sheetrock, cables, paint cans and a luscious assortment of workmen, sensing she's mired in a black hole of final preparations and isn't going to take this surprise visit well.

"I'm always the bearer of bad news!" he announces out loud. Smacks lighting guy on the ass as he passes.

"Crab. I said crab!" Sadie yells at the caterer over the phone.

"Ooo, you or him?" Julio says swinging around the desk to read over her shoulder.

Sadie looks up, points to the door, "Get lost … No! not you. I'm talking to someone else, look …" Snaps her fingers at the door.

"Chew choo hear this," Julio cautions, jerks his head away from her violent finger snapping above her head. "No, chew gonna wanna hear this, Ms. Sadie."

"If it's too much for you to handle, then I'll find someone else …" swivels around in the chair, "Go now … No not you! Hold on," presses the phone to her chest, "Are you crazy? What is it?"

"Your friendly competitor is sneaking around the gallery. Her face look shrink wrap," pulls his cheeks tight, "I don know how she can breed this way."

Sadie squeezes her eyes shut, takes a deep breath, and puts the phone back to her ear, "Just see what you can come up with. If it isn't ready tomorrow, I'll find someone who can handle the order." Plunks the phone back in the cradle. "Like I can whip crab out of my ass! So, what does Lydia want?"

"I no talk to her, chew know? I just the messenger, or passenger pigeon, or whatever." He starts massaging Sadie's shoulders. Feels her melt under his hands. Learned the value of this little trick two days after being hired as her assistant.

"What am I going to do about her? Harder."

"Chew could tell her to leaf, but aren't chew curious why chee is here?"

"I know why. She didn't get a damn invitation," drops her head. "Maybe I'll tell her she can come. What can she do at this point anyway?"

"Do what chew want. Just don't touch her. Chee might *pop!*"

"God, Julio. You're just weird," Sadie says, squirming out of the chair.

It does set Sadie aback. Just for a moment. Julio didn't exaggerate. Poor thing is stretched a little tight ... But not from Botox. "That's a face lift," Sadie whispers to Julio, "and a bad one. Always was a cheap old bitch."

Julio shakes his head and disappears into the back room.

"And what brings you to this side of town?" Sadie smiles, suspecting Lydia can't exactly smile back.

"Nice place," Lydia turns, "and I am only three blocks away, dear." Runs her hand along the metal frame of an abstract by the door. "Are these the entries for your little contest?"

Sadie takes it as an insult. Sounds like an insult. "We've had a nice turn out. Lamont is so pleased with the outcome."

"Really? And how old is he now? Heard he was suffering from Alzheimer's."

"That's petty, Lydia. Even for you. He's arranging for the winner to get a showing at Art Basel Miami."

"Well, good luck getting an unknown into Basel, dear."

"How's your gallery going, Lydia?"

Sadie and Lydia switch places like swordsmen at the start of a fencing match. From the reaction on Lydia's face, the arch in her eyebrow, far too high now on the forehead, Sadie knows she's scored a point.

"Excellent. Best year yet. Antonio sends his regards."

Like hell, Sadie thinks. Flashbacks to the day Antonio left her. Hot young Latin Antonio. Fifteen years her junior. Antonio who took his work with him and offered it to her competitor.

She could handle the breakup. But the loss of his work at her gallery had almost sunk her. More emotionally than financially. She loves his work. Maybe loved the work more than the man himself.

"He does excellent work. He sent in a piece. There on the wall. I remember when he painted it. One of those lazy Sunday mornings we stayed in bed. He got a sudden inspiration."

"Really? Well, from what I can see, it looks like he's a shoo in."

Sadie leans in close. "You know, I thought so too, but then," moves closer so she can see the tiny scalp scars from the surgery through Lydia's thinning hair. Tries not to stare. "The very last box. The very last box I'm telling you, had such a surprise, well, I couldn't speak. I just couldn't speak."

"It must have been something if you couldn't talk, dear." Lydia says sarcastically.

"I know! But I've got to say, Antonio is in for a run for his money." Places her hand on Lydia's boney elbow and ushers her to the last room in the gallery.

"What do you think?"

Lydia doesn't speak. She stands rigid trying to process what's in front of her. Her heart sinks. She moves closer to the prints lined along the floor as final preparations are made on their mounting clips. She slowly bends at the waist to read the signature.

"Who's the artist?"

"Joseph Salas."

Lydia nods. Slowly. "That's what I thought it said."

"Lives right here in town. Under our noses the whole time. Who knew?"

"Who knew indeed? Have you actually met him, dear?"

"When he brought them in and filled out the forms. Nice gentleman." Bites her lip, "Why don't you drop by for the gala, Lydia?"

"Yes, I just might. Antonio has been begging me to go with him."

"Must be getting desperate," Sadie mutters over her shoulder.

"Well dear, what I always say, don't count your chickens before they're hatched." Lydia straightens up, slaps her hand on her chest as if checking her heart rate. Takes note of the phone number on Joe's entry. Eyes glint in the low light.

29

and the winner is...

TWENTY-FOUR HOURS later, Joe gets the call. He's told that he's placed first and is expected to attend the formal gala the following Saturday night. Even though he hears it all, he can't comprehend it. It feels surreal and he's not sure what he's supposed to do with the news.

Pop's half twisted out of the recliner, eavesdropping. Can't tell from Joe's expression if it's good news or not. That always irritated him about the boy. Knows it's important by the way Joe chews at his fingers. "Well?"

Joe slowly looks down at him, mouths words without volume. Pop turns up his hearing aid. "What? Can't hear you."

Joe just stares at him.

"I said I can't hear you. What?"

"I won."

"Won what?"

"The art contest. Placed first. Gonna be a big fancy gala on Saturday."

"You mean the place down there? Where you dropped off the boxes?"

"Yeah. Got a good suit?"

"Why?"

"Need a date."

"And I'm the best you can come up with?"

"Pretty much. Wanna go or not?"

"Means I'll have to take a bath. Shave too," leans forward, rubs his stubbly chin, and looks to the bathroom. "Well, I was planning to wash on Saturday anyway." Pulls himself out of the chair.

"Where you goin'?"

"See what still fits."

"It's not tonight, Pop. You got a few days."

"Better to be prepared. What I always say," Pop says limping down the hall. Shuffles a little half-assed jig as soon as he's alone in his room.

30

you really don't want to know

LYDIA'S ALL A titter behind the wheel of her '95 Caddie, her grip, eight knuckle bones desperate to tear through thin skin, squeezed as if around Sadie's neck.

It's the remark about Antonio and Sadie's lazy Sunday afternoons, and the innuendo of great sex that replays in her mind like a radio with an obnoxious DJ that just won't shut up. As if he knows she hasn't had great sex in …yeah, that long.

She glances at the small shred of tissue between her fingers, Joe's phone number hastily written on it before anyone noticed. Sadie would have known immediately what was up her sleeve if she'd been caught. Might have intervened and called Joe to warn him. Then her mind switches back to Antonio, her brain intercutting two prominent images: Antonio turning on her and going back to Sadie, and Joe laughing because he was sleeping with Sadie, too.

She barrels down the gallery driveway spattering loose gravel against the car frame and slides to a stop. Just barely taps the garage door with the bumper.

Keys in hand, she hurries into her office and dials the number on the soggy tissue decomposing in her hand. A man with the inflection and quiver in his voice like an old guy trying to choke out difficult words says something that isn't hello.

"May I speak to Joseph Salas, please?"

"Who is it?"

"I'm from the gallery. Is he in?" Cranky bastard, she thinks.

"Oh? Yeah! Just a minute, there."

Lydia hears the phone rattle, probably put down. Muffled voices. Wonders if Joe's been standing there the whole-time screening calls.

"Joe Salas."

"Yes, Joe, it's Lydia. I just wanted to congratulate you on your win. Now before you hang up on me, I just wanted to say how sorry I am for the way we left things. I just wasn't aware how tormented you were."

"What do you want?"

"I have a proposition for you and wonder if I could ask you to come by the gallery this evening? I also have your severance check." Thinks that'll get him in if nothing else. Holds her breath. Doesn't realize she's grinning as if he were right in front of her.

A long silence. She imagines him standing with the phone to his ear trying to verbalize a way to turn her down. Half expects him to cuss her out and hang up. Her grin stretches into a lopsided sneer as her hand rests on her chest. She feels her heartbeat fluttering against her palm as if she'd caught a lizard. "Are you still there, Joe?"

"Can make it around nine."

It takes her a second to realize he's accepted the invitation and since passed the conversation back to her. "Wonderful! Nine then." Hangs up and her mind immediately jumps to a plan of attack that would be the envy of any field officer. "Glory!" she yells. Visions of fame and fortune dance before her eyes. Then she wonders, for just a moment, if he's still unstable. Thinks surely, he must be past it. Sadie didn't mention anything about his peculiarities, but the poor girl doesn't know him all that well, does she?

Money. She needs to cut a check. But for how much? Severance her ass. If she has to buy him, who cares? Free enterprise is what it is. "Smart girl, Lydia."

HE WAS GOING to just ride his bike over, then decides at the last minute to take the Buick. Needs to stop at the grocery before going home. Kill two birds with one stone.

The old gallery broods on its corner lot in the dark. And other than a different featured artist on the sign in the lit window, the place looks about the same as when he left. Fired. Didn't leave. Was fired. Needs to remember that.

Joe drives around to the back, sees Lydia's Caddie parked in front of the garage and slides in next to it.

Lydia hears a car moving over the gravel around back, goes to the hall mirror to check her face. Looks at her hairline, wonders if Sadie noticed the scars. Maybe not. She begins to open the door before he knocks and decides it will make her appear too hungry. Yeah, she is, but might not be such a good idea, looking that hungry.

She waits, leans to the door listening for his footsteps on the back stairs, rehearsing what she's going to say, editing the language to simple words. No confusing legal stuff. At least until she hands him an exclusive contract. Right after the phony severance check. Pretty sure Sadie hasn't signed him yet. She surely would've mentioned it, and couldn't have helped bragging about it. That's what she plans to do the moment Joe's signature dries on the dotted line. Call her up…No, not call. Go over there! Yes! Let the little bitch read it and weep.

A knock on the door and she jumps. Adrenaline sears her chest. She smoothes the front of her sweater, repositions her ill-fitting shoe, and opens the door.

He stands on the top step. Doesn't say a word. She thinks he was never socialized as a kid, remembers that realization shortly after hiring him. Couldn't put him in charge of anything that placed him on a one to one basis with the public. He'd stand looking at them, waiting. They'd stand looking back, waiting, until they got uncomfortable enough to excuse themselves. No chit chat. No conversation. They'd ask questions and get one-word answers. And leave. With their money.

Her featured artists got a little more from him. Offensive gestures in the hall. So, she was told. She feared Joe enough not to tell him his work just didn't measure up. Too crude. Like him. Crude. She did lead him on in hopes of a showing, but she was right, he wasn't ready. Hopes he's gotten over it all, realized she was right in the long run. Hell, she discovered him. Only right she gets to keep him.

"Joe! So nice to see you. I'm thrilled you could come by on such short notice," she says, aware it sounds a little cheesy. He stands on the step and just looks at her until motivated by her gesture to enter.

"Got my check?"

Question's a little cold, she thinks. Not out of character, though. Tries to shed his eyes as he moves into the room. They're still on her when she closes the door. Gooseflesh rises across her shoulders in ripples.

"Absolutely. Come into the office so we can talk," she tells him rubbing her arms as if to warm up. "Can I get you coffee? Tea?"

"What's the deal?" Joe glances around the room, plops down on an antique wing chair in front of her desk, ignoring her offer of refreshment.

"For what, dear?" Lydia asks confused. She really is. Not a clue. Wonders if he somehow suspects her plans.

"The check. What's the deal with the check? Didn't think I was gettin' one."

Lydia stretches her neck and lays her hand to her chest. "You didn't? Oh, no. You left so suddenly, I didn't get your new address. I couldn't find you, dear."

Joe sits forward, props his elbows on the top of his knees, "Didn't leave. Was fired. How I remember it." Digs a mint out of one of the little leather bags on his belt and pops it in his mouth.

"Well, technically, yes," she says shaking her head. "But you left me with no other option, Joe. You embarrassed me, the gallery, and yourself. What was I to do?"

"How 'bout my damn showing? I brought 'em in and laid 'em down on the floor and you wouldn't even look at 'em." He straightens up at the waist, the mint rolling around his tongue. "You, you, walked on 'em. Left foot prints on the best one," he says agitated. "So, I burned 'em."

Lydia leans across the desk and extends her hand, willing the tremble to stop. "I am sorry, Joe. It was rude of me. Inexcusable. It was, surely, and I do hope you'll forgive me."

He doesn't take her hand, but scowls at her with obvious contempt. Snaps the mint in half with his front teeth.

She withdraws her hand and wipes it on her thigh before sitting down. Lydia opens the check book and fills one out. Rips it from the binding and slides it across the desk. He slaps his hand on top and sweeps it off. Gives it a good read through like he's expecting a counterfeit. What it looks like. First time since he got here he wasn't glaring at her. She sucks in a deep breath.

"What's the deal?" he asks. Rolls the check into a tube and tucks it into one of his little bags.

"Deal?" There it is again. That lack of communication. As if they're speaking different languages. Lydia riffles through her vocabulary searching for something to define his meaning. "I'm not following, dear."

"A proposal. Said it when you called. What is it?"

Lydia's heart jumps. "Yes, I did. Well, as you know, I have the oldest and most well-established gallery in the county and represent several successful artists. I want you to become part of our team. I feel you've come a long way in maturing your work. I know you've worked hard. A process all artists must endure to get to the point you are now. I don't think you understood or appreciated it back then."

"Don't think you did," he snaps back.

This isn't going well. Lydia senses him becoming more adversarial. "What inspired you? The work I mean. It's so unusual. I must know your technique."

"You really don't want to know."

"I really do!"

"No, you really don't."

She opens her mouth to counter, but from the look in his eye, knows not to pursue it. Shifts uncomfortably in her chair. "Can I get you a brandy perhaps?" God knows she needs one, and pulls a bottle and two glasses from her desk drawer. Fills one glass and offers it to Joe.

He waves it off, "Why the offer now?"

Lydia swallows, lets the burn pass, and sets the empty glass on the desk. "It's time to show the world your talent!" Says it like it's a news flash—fake excitement in her eyes, an undeveloped smile pulling her lips apart.

"I'm already doing that. Going to Miami."

"Really? Isn't that nice." She feels him slipping away. "It is a wonderful opportunity. But it's important you have

208

experienced representation too. It's difficult to find that. As you know, I have years and years of experience. I'm able to guide you through all the nuances of a very competitive business, you see."

"Don't think I'm interested, Queenie. My Pop sends his regards. Says thanks for the message about his accident."

Lydia tilts her head, "Queenie?"

"You don't want to know that, either."

"I don't see the point in holding grudges, do you? I think we are way beyond that now. We …"

"I'm not interested in signing anything with you," he interrupts. "I'd burn it again first." Joe stands up and turns for the door.

"Well, that's unfortunate, Joe," she says raising her voice. What a moment ago was trepidation suddenly turns malicious.

"The committee in Miami is going to frown on your poor behavior here. Mr. Novello sits on that board. You remember Mr. Novello, don't you?" Tilts her head, places her finger to her chin. "Accused him of … what was the offense you used … forgery?" Lydia moves around the desk, folds her arms.

"We're very close. Maybe you forgot." Bats her fake black gooey eyelashes. She's not about to let Sadie walk away with the best thing that's come along in years.

"I'll let Sadie know what she's facing when she gets the call from Miami declining your showing. And they will decline it." She squeezes out a little rat-mouth smile.

Joe stops with his hand on the door frame. Stands for several seconds until Lydia thinks something might be wrong, like maybe he's suddenly taken ill. A satisfying thought.

Her arms drop to her side as the old grandfather clock in the hall chimes the half hour, and Joe moves slightly, just in the shoulders, as if he might turn around, but doesn't. She starts

209

noticing the little details on the back of his neck—his long gray hair pulled to a pony tail, the shiny bald spot, the skin tag seated between his neck and shoulder. The rapid pulse in his neck.

"You want to rethink that threat?" he finally asks.

"No threat. Business."

"What do you want from me?"

"I don't want anything. Not now. It probably wouldn't have worked out anyway. Have a nice life." She turns back to her desk, self-satisfied that if she can't have him, no one can.

Joe looks over his shoulder. Checks his watch.

It comes as a quick hug, at least that's what first crosses her mind. More like a bear hug. She can feel his body against her back, his strong arms squeezing hers against her torso so that he has her pinned. She's lifted off her feet, losing her ill-fitting shoe. Struggles to keep her balance and kicks the shoe under her desk. She's tipped backward, confused. Fears falling. In an instant it hits her and the fear morphs into a thick panic. She tries to scream through mint-fragranced fingers. Tastes the acrid burn of his sweat on her tongue. His arm moves under her chin. She feels the pressure of his forearm crushing against her windpipe. His hot breath sweeps her forehead—it's all she can breathe. No air but *his* air—light blurs gray around the edges. Her eyes burn. Tingling in the back of her neck. Loss of feeling in the extremities. Grays darken. Desperate useless breaths. Her chest heaves. Pinpoint light— Blackness.

Joe's upper body shudders squeezing the life out of Lydia. She slides to the floor against his legs—him exhaling hard enough to moan, exhausted, waiting for the burn in his shoulders and forearms to subside.

She flops onto the hardwood. He steps over to the desk and notes the check book, sees she hadn't filled out her portion. Gonna need to burn the check. Plucks a tissue from the box on her desk and uses it to place the second glass back in the

210

drawer. Leaves the one she used. Rubs down the chair arms and tucks the tissue in his pocket.

Checks his watch. Nine forty-five. A good hour in a small town, he thinks. Won't be much traffic.

Joe opens the trunk of the Buick and goes back inside. Sweeps Lydia's shoe from under the desk, picks her off the floor, and carries her to the car.

Trunk dumping. Realizes he's been doing a lot of that. Makes him think it should be the title of a country song. Drops the shoe on top and shuts the trunk. He closes the gallery door, gets in the car, and drives slowly down the dark gravel drive.

31

no coupons

JOE TAKES HIS time perusing the grocery aisles. Compares the price of brand name cereal to the store brand. Save thirty cents on the store brand this week. Plunks two boxes in the cart. Milk's not such a bargain. Usually isn't.

He wanders to the meat counter. He hates the meat counter. Thinks the meat folks are too proud of their cuts. *They want an arm and leg for 'em. Jeez, gonna eat 'em, not invest in 'em! Even chuck's high this week.* Picks up some thin minute steaks and drops them in the cart.

Slides up to chicken. Chicken's high too, but they got a special on thighs. Joe drops three packs in the cart, moves on to the cleaning product aisle. He picks up a box of black construction bags, 3.00 mill. Heavier than what he'd been using. Price is higher, but thinks it's worth the cost. A blowout now could prove problematic.

He massages the soreness in his upper right arm as he guides the cart to checkout. Chats with the clerk. Gives her a friendly smile and tells her to have a nice night.

Joe opens the trunk and lays the plastic bags of groceries around Lydia. Closes it. Turns the radio to a country station and drives home.

"Got some of them minute steaks you like," Joe yells from the kitchen. Slings the meat in the fridge and grabs a beer. "Got a lemon cake."

Takes the beer and walks into the living room where Pop's on his hands and knees in front of his recliner scraping the carpet with a butter knife.

"Good for you," Pop says.

"Whatcha doin' there?"

"Got somethin' stuck to the floor here. Sap." Scrapes harder.

Joe moves to the sofa. "Where'd it come from?"

"Who the hell knows? Maybe from that pine in Dee Dee's yard. Nasty tree. Bleeds on everything. Get me some ice, will ya?"

Joe goes to the kitchen and returns with three cubes of ice. Hands them down to Pop. "Could be gum."

"It's sap." Pushes an ice cube on the spot.

"Probably gum."

Pop leans down and sniffs the spot. "Not gum. Sap."

"How can you tell?"

"'Cause you can smell it W*ho-Ass.* Sniff yourself if you don't believe me."

"If you say so, Pop." Joe grabs the phone, dials a number, and watches Pop pick at the sap with the knife again.

"Sadie? Joe Salas. I'll have another print for the Miami showing. That be okay, or is it too late?"

Pop stops scraping. Slowly raises his head.

"Tomorrow? Yeah, I guess it can be ready for tomorrow. Thanks." Joe hangs up and grabs his beer off the coffee table. Sees Pop's staring at him. "What?"

Pop examines the spot as if it's important. "Guess you'll be in late tonight." He peels the sap from the carpet, sticks it in a tissue and painfully crawls back into the recliner.

"Not too late. We'll go get a breakfast in the morning, how's that?"

Pop nods. It's all he can force himself to do.

32

ladies night

DEE DEE'S LIGHTS go out about midnight. Joe slips out of the house and walks up and down the sidewalk to be sure, notes the half-moon struggling through broken cloud cover, air pregnant with rain. Hopes he can do without a flashlight.

Lydia's easier to move than the boys. Slings her rug-like over his shoulder and carries her through the back yard to the shed, unlocks it, and lays her on the floor.

The art tools are eager, lined up on one end of the bench: two-inch brushes, India ink, tubes of acrylics, rolls of crisp white paper. Ornate frames stacked in the corner mimic their future companion mats hanging from a hook over the vice-grip. Clearance sale stuff.

Joe stands over the body a good fifteen minutes thinking of how he wants to dress the print. Considers how Lydia wants her image to look to the world. Her features were important to her. Anyone who knew her, knew that. Then an idea hits him and he wonders if he's got enough black paint.

DEE DEE STARTS to close the vertical blinds on the kitchen sliders when she sees light bleed through the boards of the Salas's shed. First time since she's been back she's noticed any activity at night.

She'd sat in a lawn chair yesterday with the sliders open, shelling boiled peanuts, listening to Pop putter in and out of the shed, fartin' around with his plants.

Cops and doctors almost had her convinced the whole episode in the shed was a hallucination. Almost. The prickling beneath her skin insists it's not in her head. Something's just not right about the place. But she needs evidence if she's gonna prove them wrong—like shoving photos of his mass slaughter in their faces and force them to apologize for doubting her. A sweet wonder. But there's that trespass warning. That little stained piece of paper curled next to the coffee maker reminding her she can't go in the Salas's yard anymore.

"Could go to jail," cop warned. "Can kiss my black ass," she'd snapped back as the cop handed her over to the two nice gentlemen in white coats.

She reaches into the drawer by the kitchen sink and takes out a little disposable, twelve exposure camera and stands by the sliders watching the shed. Wonders how long she should wait. Decides just long enough to finish this last cigarette.

TWO SHEETS OF paper covered in black paint dry on a makeshift line hung across the shed. Lydia's seated, propped against the bench, hands folded neatly in her lap, head slumped on her left shoulder. Like she'd sported binge drinking and passed out. Makes Joe smile thinking about Lydia being lit, imagining her dancing on the bench, whooping it up.

He pours an opaque paint mixed with glaze in a small paper plate then sits on the floor next to her. He folds his arms over his propped knees carefully studying her profile both left and right.

"This was a shitty way to end it, Queenie." Gently brushes her tight cheek with back of his hand, fascinated how stretched the corners of her mouth are. Pokes at her fuchsia lips. Mom comes to mind, an intrusion, like she did when he was fourteen—coming into his bedroom and catching him stretched across the bed with a box of tissue, deep in the rhythm. She did it twice. She'd made a big deal of it, got Pop involved, made him "counsel" the sin of it all.

As if alive, her voice, scattered in the deep recesses of his mind, invades, *"It's a sin, Joe. Don't you know?"* He'd never considered the right or wrong of it, not consciously. A means to an end. A problem solved. Like the killing of Keys. An accident, he knows that, but dead just the same.

Ricky, well, he had it coming. Even Mom would have to agree considering the horrors inflicted on Betty and his kid. Anyone in their right mind would agree. But, Lydia here, she's a different kind of killing. And he suddenly chills at the realization, a bad one, an unnecessary one. Had he been hasty? Mom would've called it hasty, not thinking the problem through like she'd accused him of not doing so many times. He squelches a pang of regret and reminds himself of what was at stake allowing her to live.

"Just stay out of it!"

Lydia's face becomes Mom's face, and for an instant fears he's killed her, strangled her by indifference with the pettiness of his hands. Had she been the first, the true first in his collection? Even now, Lydia sneers, as if mocking.

The tips of his fingers trace her bone structure all the way to the hairline, notices small incision marks from the surgeon's scalpel, decides right is her best side. He lays her on her left, tucking old bath towels around her neck to keep her head from shifting during the process.

217

He lays one of the dried papers on the floor, dips the brush into the paint, gently scraping off the excess on the lip of the plate. Draws the brush over her skin.

"We'll just think of this as one of those new age facials. Sorry, don't have music or candles."

It takes less than an hour to coat and print the face twice, sticking pins through the paper into the flesh for stability.

After removal, he examines the print with a magnifying glass to see if there is sufficient detail. It looks good. He places one print on the bench, hangs the second on the line above her, and as they dry, pours adhesive into another paper plate. Plucks a small artists detail brush from the holder and dips it in the adhesive and applies it to any painted area. He unfolds thin sheets of genuine gold leaf and lays it on the adhesive. Taps it in with a soft bristle brush.

"My best idea yet," he tells her. "My golden Queen Cleopatra."

He allows a good ten minutes for the adhesive to dry, checks his watch, thinks about going to the house for a beer. Figures he'll wait and see how the whole thing turns out first.

NO MUU MUU. Ironed shorts, sweatshirt, sandals. And the camera clutched in her sweaty palm, her thumb rubbing over the advance wheel. Hopes she remembers to advance each shot, but might not have much time.

Dee Dee slowly slides open the glass doors to the patio where a light drizzle coats the yard and concrete. She considers getting a jacket, maybe one with a hood. No time. Flicks the cigarette filter in the dark. She crouches, watches the fence, and creeps to the palmetto palm that's sprung from the ground seemingly overnight. She pushes the four wide fronds aside to see through the slats.

WITH A SOFT bristle brush, Joe sweeps away any gold leafing not in the adhesive. As the brush strokes the gold, a shape begins to emerge, a distinct profile, eye socket, brow bone, outer ear. Flecks of gold leaf float to the floor and collect like glitter on the tops of his thighs.

Lydia's image is unfolding, as if a butterfly from its pupa, growing more detailed with each stroke. He uses a sable spotter to gently set the fine lines, blowing away excess leafing from the paper with a soft breath. Clips the print to the door and stands back chewing at his paint-coated thumb nail.

"Lookin' good, Queenie." Throws a towel over Lydia's head. "Getting a beer. Be back."

DEE DEE WATCHES him leave, sees he's left the light on. Just like before. She pulls the camera to her face and gets it in position. Doesn't want to fumble with it, needs that quick shoot and scoot. They'll have to believe her with cold hard pictures. Might get her picture in the paper. Maybe TV. Imagines standing with reporters, giving them a blow by blow account of how she caught a serial killer single handed.

The moment she hears Joe's back door close, she springs to her feet and makes her way out the gate and into the Salas's back yard. She scuttles down the fence line and slips behind the shed into a shadow cast by the Drake Elm under an anemic moon. Threads of wet hair cling to her face.

Standing on her toes, she angles her head to better spy through shrunken boards, swipes hair from her eyes. Can't see much—corner of the bench, garden tools, push mower, and … thinks they're feet. She pulls a cement block over to stand on for more height. Damn! Still can't see. She hops off, glances at Joe's back door. Hurries to the shed door and slips inside.

Sprawled legs with stockings. She can see the linear run from the calf to the ankle. Bare painted toes poke through the ruptured nylons. Nice print skirt, soiled on the right side. Sweater, hoisted up under the bra. Head, towel covered.

Dee Dee tip-toes to the bench. She forgets about the camera in her sweaty palm. Her fingers tremble reaching for the towel and delicately lifts one corner with a thumb and forefinger. Sees a chin. Bottom lip. Mouth, open slightly. She lifts the towel.

Lydia's eyes pop open, the black mascara spread like bruises and running down one cheek, one half of her face painted black. The old woman gasps for breath. Her hand clamps down on Dee Dee's arm.

Dee Dee shrieks, struggles to peel off Lydia's fingers.

Lydia's mouth stretches against the numbing toxin in her muscles and gags, her desperate eyes pleading.

Dee Dee pulls from Lydia's grip, stumbles and falls. She suddenly remembers the camera and squeezes the shutter release. *Flash.*

Lydia gropes the air after her.

Dee Dee advances the wheel for another shot and backs into Joe's legs. The camera flash goes off again.

Joe grabs her wet hair. "What's it gonna take to get rid of you!?"

Lydia's eyes follow him around the room, mouthing silent screams as he wrestles his neighbor.

Joe grabs a hammer off the bench and swings. Just misses Dee Dee's head. He loses his balance and falls to the floor on his hands. Gives Dee Dee time to scramble through the shed door. Joe launches after her.

Dee Dee can hear him moving up behind her and makes the mistake of looking over her shoulder and trips. Takes a hard fall into the fence. She stupidly thinks of all the horror movies where the girl runs, trips, and predictably gets slaughtered. Wood splinters dig into her palms and scrub the skin off the tip of her nose.

In an instant, he's on top of her, all his weight, wiry strands of hair pulled from the rubber band spiraling from the sides of his head, hands slick and useless. And although her sweatshirt gives him substance, her kick in his gut forces him to breathlessly reconsider long enough for her to get to her feet and run through the gate. But he's only four steps behind. She tries a zigzag maneuver learned watching football—gives her the extra seconds to make it to the sliders.

Joe leaps forward, slips in the wet grass, and trips over the creepy garden gnome. Feels like it's gonna leave a nice bruise on the shin bone. And she's in the house and locked the slider before he can get to his feet, watches the vertical blinds flip close.

"*Shit!*" he bellows. Kicks a plastic lawn chair across the yard.

Gotta get rid of Lydia before the cops show, he tells himself as he limps through the yard worrying how much time he has. Probably not much.

But Lydia's gone. Grabbing the flashlight, Joe runs through the backyard gritting his teeth, light beam sweeping hedges and the fence line. Thinks she might try for the car, maybe the street, has a horrible image of her banging on neighbor's doors begging for help, or screaming in the middle of the street until someone calls the cops. Lucky for him most of his neighbors are still up north, their vacant homes nothing more than mute witnesses.

Tricky girl she's turned out to be and he wonders what it takes to squeeze people to death. He clearly didn't squeeze hard enough. He's glad he got two prints from her. He's sure killing her a second time will be messy.

Twenty minutes of searching and Joe finds Lydia by the gate to the pond barely breathing. He must have just crippled her. She's kind of pathetic crumpled in a heap in Pop's daylily bed, legs splayed between the *Mardi Gras Parade* and the *Red Hot Returns*. Joe stands over her shaking his head as if she were a child caught with new bag of cookies and had snuck off to eat 'em all.

"Stupid woman, Queenie. Should've stayed dead."

One of the new heavy mill garbage bags and the tarp are thrown out the shed door. And the more Joe thinks about Lydia, the more pissed he gets. "Should've stayed out of my business," he mutters, drawing the machete from its sheath. Runs the blade across the whet stone six or seven times and turns off the light. Mom's face, like a hollow echo, penetrates his consciousness again as if it's her going under the blade. *"It's a sin, Joe! Don't you know?"*

Lydia's rolled up in the tarp like a burrito. He slings her over his shoulder and totes her down to the pond. Before he can get his tools together, blue strobe lights reflect over the rooftops. First time he's ever felt the spark of panic. Wishes it was Dee Dee wrapped in the tarp more than Lydia.

By the time Joe gets to the back door, cops are at the front door talking to Pop. He pulls a beer from the fridge and walks into the living room as if cops are there for weekly poker night. Come by frequently enough he recognizes the big one. Has a different partner with him. A seedy little guy, a real runt compared to the others.

"Cops here again," Pop says.

"Yeah, I see that, Pop." He waves and takes another swallow of beer. "Get you officers anything?"

Cop One declines, hands Runty Cop paperwork.

Pop leans over to read it. "She's at it again, JoJo. Nosey bitch. How many reports that make this year?" Elbows Runty

Cop in the side and limps back to his recliner. "Gonna start charging you boys rent."

Cop One asks, "You kill anyone tonight, Mr. Salas?" Just like that.

"No. What's going on?" Joe sits on the arm of the sofa and sets his beer down. Won't look at Pop. "This about her again?"

Cop One nods. "Says you have a woman in your shed."

"Really? Woman this time?" Joe glances at Pop but doesn't make eye contact. Thinks the cops will see the deception between them.

Pop leans over the arm of his recliner and wiggles his finger at Joe, "You can bring 'em in the house, boy. No need to sneak around in the shed with your girlfriends. You're an adult now." Grins.

"Thanks, Pop. Shed's this way." Joe says. Hands Pop his walkin' stick, doesn't wait to ask if they want to see the shed, just moves through the house to the back door.

Pop pokes Joe in the ass with his stick, "Maybe she's jealous. Got the hots for ya. Maybe you should take her out on a date!"

Joe pushes off the stick. "Stop it. It's not funny."

Pop pokes him again, "Is too."

Dee Dee's back porch light is on. She's pacing the patio, straining to see shadows of people moving around the shed. She has a tight grip on the camera, waiting for the moment she can shove it at the cop and make him admit he was wrong.

Joe opens the shed and turns on the light just as a misty drizzle begins to fall again.

Pop shuffles back to the house to watch from the back door so he doesn't get wet.

Joe worries about Lydia, half dead by the pond, and fears what will happen if she were to free herself again and just show up. He imagines her telling the cops about how he tried to strangle her then dragged her to this place to use her face for some kind of sick art project. She'd point to the bruises on her throat and the needle marks—corroborate what Dee Dee had been accusing him of all this time.

"Have you, Mr. Salas?" Cop One asks.

Joe doesn't hear the question. Takes him a moment to realize it. "Excuse me?"

"Have you been down here tonight?"

"Yeah. Been working on another art piece for the gallery," he says pointing to the exotic gold print drying on the makeshift line. "How long am I gonna have to put up with this?" He notices Runty Cop poking around the back yard with a Maglite.

"I'm going to go talk to her. If I have anything else, I'll be back." Cop One joins Runty Cop for a short conversation then leaves for Dee Dee's place.

Joe turns off the light and locks the shed, watches Runty Cop turn and look beyond the back gate.

"What's back there?" cop asks. Tilts his head as if he's caught the potent scent of death. Steps closer to the gate, the Maglite beam sweeping the edge of the woods line.

"Artesian pond. Muck. Woods. Saw a bobcat once," Joe says.

"How far back does it go?"

"Miles, I suppose. Wanna go down?" Joe waits for an answer, unaware how shallow he's breathing, but Runty Cop's radio chatters a series of numbers and evidently, it's for him because he turns off his Maglite and hurries out of the yard.

Joe's not sure what he would've done if the cop wanted to go down. Lead him anywhere except where the body is, he supposes. Joe goes into the house and grabs another beer.

Pop quick limps in, waving him over. "You'll wanna see this, boy. They got a good fight on their hands now," he yells turning back for the living room.

In her front yard, Dee Dee's released a litany of profanity that sounds more like a foreign language. Runty Cop grabs her left wrist and meets her right fist in the face. Knocks him on his ass. Cop One, arms crossed over his chest, watches Runty recover and take a second stab at her. Weaving and ducking, Runty gets one handcuff on, but can't get on the second. They play tug-of-war, her spinning him in a circle by her sheer weight, his feet sliding out from under him.

"She's kickin' his ass!" Pop yells from the doorway, jumping and thrusting his arms out as if he's in the fight. Scares Joe a little seeing how excited Pop is.

"Pussy Boy!" Pop yells. "You gonna let a girl kick your ass, *pussy boy?!"*

Reminds Joe of the Pop from his childhood.

As much fun as it is to watch, Cop One puts an end to it. He steps up and grabs Dee Dee by the wrist and upper arm and twists her to the ground. Face first.

Secured, Runty Cop leads her to the patrol car and stuffs her in the back. Slams the door. Sulks back to the yard to retrieve his radio. And his report holder. And his pen. And the badge she ripped from his shirt.

Cop One walks back to the Salas's front porch, excitement still pungent.

"That's one nasty bitch," Pop says limping back in the house. "Told you so, too."

Joe steps out. "What happened?"

"She admitted snooping around your shed. That violated her trespass warning. I suspected that when she called in the complaint. Battery on a law enforcement officer got her a felony."

"Taking her back to the nut house?"

"Nope. This time she goes to jail. The judge will probably have her reevaluated."

"Your partner there all right?"

Cop One smiles. "Trainee. His first arrest." Shakes his head and hands Joe paper to sign. Joe scribbles his name and hands it back.

"You folks have a nice night," Cop says, stepping into the yard.

33

a perfect execution

LYDIA DIES ROLLED in the tarp. And even though it was his intention, her death fails to elate him. Joe feels sad her dying this way, out in the Florida wilds alone, yet struggles with relief. He wasn't looking forward to killing her again.

On his hands and knees, he carefully unwraps the tarp, picks dried vegetation from her sweater. He brushes hair from the black streaks under her fixed stare, lies down and spoons against her back until the last of her body heat seeps into the night air.

He thinks he shouldn't leave her lying out here like this, so whole. Where things bite and gnaw. It's stupid. She's dead. She won't feel any of it.

Much of the next hour is a blur. Numb and cold inside, he ceases conscious thought while cleaning the machete and putting away the tools and tarp. Throws the garbage bag with Lydia's clothing in the can.

In the bathroom, he looks at his reflection, blood peppered across his face and shirt. He reaches into the medicine cabinet for relief from the headache that throbs deep in his temple and Mom's face cream rebukes him. *"It's a sin, Joe!"* He wipes his face and pukes.

AND ON THE wall, lit by warm recesses, their faces, an exhibited moment in time, an image of death disguised in metallic colors of copper, bronze and green, with trace gilding in gold leaf. A mask before critics, unknown, as their identities lay decayed among the pines. Expressions on rice paper, stripped from their host, their black inked details bleached white on true bone. Fragrance of incense, fragrance of the pond and the thick black muck. Silenced voices.

Joe feels, in his creation, the power of life and death, feels his chest swell seeing them for the first time lined along the wall with all the excuses and all the reasons. He still hears them and knows they've been resurrected, given purpose. Given himself purpose.

Pop stands behind him dressed in the suit bought for Mom's funeral, a fresh polish to his shoes, a silk tie, mouth gaping. Lined along the wall like the remnants of an execution, they're collected, awarded blue ribbons tagged to the frames as if decorated for bravery.

One face he recognizes immediately, the aberration of his nightmares, the eye still straining to penetrate his soul. He can't look away, doesn't notice the walkin' stick trembling beneath his hand, deafened by his own breathing as if it's the only sound in the world.

"Gotta go to the car and get the other print," Joe tells him. "They got food over there. Coffee too, I think." Leaves Pop with an audience of the dead.

Pop limps from print to print. Pulls at his tie. A hand clamps down on his shoulder and he starts as if Keys has come back to reclaim his stolen life and needs to settle the score.

"What do you think?" Lamont asks, patting Pop again. "I haven't seen talent like this in years. It's so original."

Pop's unable to collect his reply, stutters an agreement hoping he's not asked to form long sentences. Vulnerable, he shakes his head and urgently looks for Joe, imagines those on the walls may be deciding his own fate. "Good," he says.

"Better than good. It's genius!" Lamont says moving past Pop and closer to a framed piece of a man looking predatorily into the eyes of a gilded woman on a copper background. "It's as if they know things we don't. Can you see it? Look at the tension. You can feel the conversation with your eyes. Fear and hate. It's all there!"

"Maybe they do," Pop says backing away.

"Yes! Exactly. How he captured that is the genius, you see. The way the colors vibrate. They seem to breathe. Outstanding."

"Didn't know my boy had it in him."

"Your boy? You're Mr. Salas's father?" Lamont looks genuinely impressed.

Pop nods. Begins to get swept away by pride denied in the early years.

Lamont puts his arm around Pop's shoulders. "Your son is going to be famous. You'll see. Once in Miami and in front of a world audience, everyone will know his work."

Pop looks up at Keys. "Feel like I already know 'em."

DETECTIVE CROY SITS in his car across the street watching a crowd gather at the gallery. On the front seat, a folder tucked in a report holder fastened to the passenger seat, neatly organized by date and case name.

The dash glistens under the streetlight from a fresh coating of Armor All, no dust in the air vents, no sand or dried vegetation on the floor mats. An air freshener hangs from the virgin cigarette lighter.

Joe exits the building and opens the trunk of the Buick.

Croy pulls out a folder, slips from the car and crosses the street. Tugs the sleeves of his dress jacket and swipes at lint.

Joe doesn't notice. Too many people around the entrance to notice one man. He pulls Lydia's print, wrapped in brown paper, from the trunk and sets it carefully on the curb.

"It looks like you've got a hit on your hands," Croy says stepping up, folder tucked under his arm.

Joe recognizes the voice. It takes him back to the killing of Ricky and that takes him back to Betty's death, heat flushing the back of his neck. "What they keep sayin'. Here for the gala, Detective Croy?"

"Among other things. Thought I'd see what the buzz is all about."

"Didn't think cops were arty types. Sports junkies from what I've seen. You know, physical action, heavy hitting." Joe smiles.

"Really? You know a lot about law enforcement, do you?"

"Not so much. Know around here jacked-up trucks with big tires are popular with 'em. The NASCAR crowd. And hunting."

Joe starts to close the trunk and notices Lydia's shoes tucked next to a cardboard box. Looks at Croy. Sees he notices them, too.

"I'm glad I ran into you actually. I have a few questions."

"I'm busy, but you probably guessed that," Joe says closing the trunk.

"Just one or two. It won't take long."

Joe picks up the print and starts walking.

"Have you heard from Mr. Vega?" Croy asks walking with him.

"Why should I?"

"Your connection to Mrs. Vega," Croy says holding open the door for Joe.

"They were divorced."

"I realize that, but I don't think Mr. Vega felt that way. See, he'd moved in her house and used her car."

"How do you know that?"

"Forensics. We processed the house and the car. His prints were all over it. As were yours. But the thing is no one's seen him since ... I talked to you."

Joe weaves his way through the well-dressed crowd trying to protect the print. "Your point, Detective?"

"Well, you said he didn't live with her, but the evidence—and it is extensive evidence Mr. Salas—that he did live there."

Joe sets the print on the floor and catches Julio's attention, waves him over. "I said she didn't have a choice. She didn't want him there. He just re-infested her life and took over. Didn't get that the first time?"

"So, you knew he was living with her?" Croy backs up as Julio hugs Joe.

"I'm going to faint, chew know? Is so exciting and chew bring another ... can wait to see it. I put it up right away," Julio says, grabbing the print and running off with it.

Joe turns back to Croy who has the folder open in his hand. "That all?"

"I'd like to show you something. See if you can make sense of it." Croy hands over the folder, a photo paper-clipped to the top.

Joe shakes his head. "Really out of focus. What is it?" Joe hands it back.

"A face. Doesn't it look like a face to you? I know it's blurry and distorted, but you can make out a definite profile." Traces a profile on the print with a manicured finger and turns it around so Joe can see it again.

Joe pretends to study it. "If you say so."

"We got this from a camera given to us by Dee Dee Turner, your neighbor. She's in jail, but you know that, right?"

"Then you know she's a wack job."

"Well, maybe, but she insists this is a picture of one of your victims."

"You mean the phantom victim the cops didn't find? Careful Detective. You're close to harassment." Looks to the back room. "Know what that's a picture of?" Joe leads Croy to the display in the packed room of glittering ball gowns and bright overhead lighting, extends his hand at the prints. "That look familiar?"

Croy pulls the photo from the folder, moves through the crowd, and holds it up to the line of prints.

"See. She got a shot of …" Joe takes the photo and eyes each print. Settles on Lydia's print freshly hung at the far end. "Her. See? I make these in the shed. Been working on 'em since the hurricane. Sound familiar?" Hands back the photo. "Check your dates. I, we," Joe pulls Pop over to join him, "live next to a crazy bitch with no life of her own."

"Talkin' about Dee Dee?" Pop asks. Can see from the tension that they are. "She's got the hots for my boy here. Won't leave him alone. Told him to take her out on a date!"

Joe sees he's made his point.

Croy looks at the print then back at the photo. Same profile but without the added metallic colors.

Julio and Sadie come up. Sadie hugs Joe and takes a glass of champagne from the waiter, hands one to Joe, Pop, and herself.

"I think we should have a toast." Taps the glass with a hors d'oeuvre fork. "Attention please!" The crowd hushes and their attention focuses on Sadie.

"I want to thank all of you for coming and making this such a success. I want to announce that Mr. Salas's work has been accepted to Art Basel Miami!"

The crowd claps and hushes again.

"A toast to the newest star of the art world." Sadie raises her glass and meets Joe's, Pop's and Julio's. The crowd claps again.

Joe takes a sip, smiling. Glances over his shoulder and sees Croy still in the audience. Croy nods.

Sadie takes Joe's arm and leads him closer to the display. The overhead lights dim leaving only somber spot lights on each print. Joe swipes the corner of his eye.

"They're fabulous," Sadie tells him, hugging his shoulder.

Julio, arm around Joe's other arm, cocks his head. "Chew know, this new one," cocks his head in the opposite direction, "Chee look so much like Ms. Lydia. No you thin, Ms. Sadie?"

Joe glances at Pop and quickly swallows what's left in his glass. Pop does the same.

RED CARNATIONS WITH baby's breath, tucked in a wide red ribbon. Joe stands over Jamie's grave, a small recently dug hole beside it.

Northern winds pull strands of hair from Joe's ponytail and stick to his cheek. The cemetery director, standing off by an older row of head stones, awaits Joe's signal.

Pop, resting his weight on his walkin' stick, holds a photo of Betty and Jamie during better times. Quickly swipes his left eye, glances to the far east end where Mom rests.

"Don't know what to say here," Joe says. Knows Pop isn't sure either. Wasn't sure the last time they stood on this ground. Neither is eloquent with speeches.

Joe kneels and places the carnations in the small brass holder at the head of the plaque. Betty's name, birth date and death date added next to Jamie's. He takes Betty's box of ashes and places it in the hole. Stands up. Nods for the cemetery director.

No big ceremony, no great crowd. No tent with chairs overwhelmed with floral spray arrangements, no grieving friends. No farewell speeches. As if Betty and Jamie had never existed.

Pop limps up and drops the photo on top of the box. He takes Joe's arm and they slowly walk back to a limo waiting to take them to Miami on a sunny, windy, Tuesday afternoon.

DETECTIVE CROY SITS across the street from the Salas's quiet home. On the front seat lie reports and the distorted photo from Dee Dee's camera. He rubs at the corners of his mouth, watching a tight kettle of vultures form in the sky and spiral from the dead pine up to the heavens.

"There will be a time to murder and create. And indeed, there will be a time to wonder."

T.S.Eliot

J L Rehman lives in the
Vanishing rurals of central
Florida with a background
In law enforcement and a
Fascination of the macabre.

Also by J L Rehman

No Middle Ground

Blood of Belladonna

Insanity Road